Hell Squad: Noah

Anna Hackett

Noah

Published by Anna Hackett
Copyright 2015 by Anna Hackett
Cover by Melody Simmons of eBookindiecovers
Edits by Tanya Saari

ISBN (eBook): 978-0-9943584-5-5
ISBN (paperback): 978-0-9945572-3-0

What readers are saying about Anna's Science Fiction Romance

At Star's End – One of Library Journal's Best E-Original Romances for 2014

Return to Dark Earth – One of Library Journal's Best E-Original Books for 2015 and two-time SFR Galaxy Awards winner

The Phoenix Adventures – SFR Galaxy Award Winner for Most Fun New Series and "Why Isn't This a Movie?" Series

Beneath a Trojan Moon – SFR Galaxy Award Winner and RWAus Ella Award Winner

Hell Squad – Amazon Bestselling Science Fiction Romance Series and SFR Galaxy Award for best Post-Apocalypse for Readers who don't like Post-Apocalypse

The Anomaly Series – #1 Amazon Action Adventure Romance Bestseller

"Like Indiana Jones meets Star Wars. A treasure hunt with a steamy romance." – SFF Dragon, review of *Among Galactic Ruins*

"Strap in, enjoy the heat of romance and the daring of this group of space travellers!" – Di, Top 500 Amazon Reviewer, review of *At Star's End*

"High action and adventure surrounding an impossible treasure hunt kept me reading until late in the night." – Jen, That's What I'm Talking About, review of *Beyond Galaxy's Edge*

"Action, danger, aliens, romance – yup, it's another great book from Anna Hackett!" – Book Gannet Reviews, review of *Hell Squad: Marcus*

Chapter One

One job down. Five hundred and seven to go.

Noah Kim ducked out of the small doorway and into the bright afternoon sun. He pressed a hidden button on the outside and watched the door—camouflaged to look like rock—slide closed. Once it was shut, there was no way to tell a secret entrance was hidden there.

He turned and started walking into the trees, headed back to Blue Mountain Base.

The secret storage facility he was working in was a ten minute walk from the main base. When they'd turned the former military base into a haven for survivors of the vicious alien invasion that had decimated Earth a year and a half ago, none of them had known this secret storage area was here.

Noah had discovered it when he and his tech team had been busy upgrading a part of the power system. He'd stumbled across old electrical cables that led in this direction from the main base. From what he could tell, the facility had housed some sort of power generator, as there were still giant turbines in place, but over the years—as energy technology increased and nuclear generators had become safe and solar-power systems viable—it had become obsolete.

The best thing about it, though, was the facility wasn't listed on Blue Mountain Base's official plans. Plans they'd recently discovered the leader of the United Coalition of Countries had sold to the aliens in return for his own safety.

Noah scowled. *Bastard.* President Howell had saved himself, and not the millions of people he'd vowed to protect. Noah stopped, forcing himself to take a second to breathe in the fresh mountain air to calm his temper. Summer was approaching, and temperatures were beginning to rise. In fact, the afternoon was hot.

Right here, right now, surrounded by the tall gum trees and hearing the rustle of small animals in the bushes and the sounds of birds overhead, Noah could almost pretend the invasion had never happened. That the dinosaur-like raptors had never arrived in their monstrous, giant spaceships and wiped out all the major cities on the planet. His gaze turned to the east, but the view was blocked by the trees. Still, he knew the ruins of Sydney were there—the once-beautiful, busy capital of the Coalition. Now, nothing more than a broken, deserted ruin.

One of those shattered skyscrapers had housed Noah's billion-dollar, online tech company. He'd always loved electronics, from the time he was old enough to tap on a comp. He'd driven his parents crazy, tinkering with things. At the age of five, he'd freaked his mother out by disassembling the toaster because it kept burning his toast. After he'd put it back together, it had worked like new. At ten, he'd pulled his father's comp apart. Noah had inherited his father's short temper. But after a fiery outburst, and after Noah added a few improvements and reassembled the comp, his dad had loved his faster device.

Noah had started work in a private R and D company in his teens, making a small fortune in salary. Then he'd started his own company, made his first million at seventeen, and his first billion at twenty-five. Kim Technology Inc. had been known as a hip, creative place to work, and a place on the cutting edge of tech. He'd been inundated by bright, young grads looking for work. Some days, he'd wished he wasn't the boss. Some days he hadn't wanted all the calls, emails, and meetings—he'd just wanted to lock himself in his tech lab and fiddle with his latest ideas.

Well, now he got to hang out in his tech lab all the time. There wasn't a whole hell of a lot of tinkering now, though. Mostly he kept the base's ventilation running, the lights on, and the hot water hot, and fixed every other damn problem the residents had. He started walking again, scraping a hand through his straight, black hair. It had gotten so long, it brushed his shoulders, something that would have given his old-fashioned grandmother heart failure.

The thought of her made him smile, and a small pain burned in his heart. God, he missed her and his parents. His Aussie mother and South Korean father had been on a vacation in South Korea, visiting his grandmother, when the aliens invaded. Some small part of him hoped they'd survived, but Seoul had been wiped out, just like every other major city around the world.

He rounded a tree and kept moving. He never used the same path to the storage facility twice. Devlin, second-in-command of the base's recon team, had scouted out a few different routes with him. Dev had warned that they couldn't risk leaving a trail the aliens could spot.

In the storage facility was the base's last hope if the aliens found them.

General Adam Holmes, head of Blue Mountain Base, was working overtime with Noah to get Operation Swift Wind organized. They had to get it operational *before* the aliens attacked.

And everyone knew it was only a matter of time.

Noah stepped into a clearing, taking a second to enjoy the sun—he missed it, being stuck underground. He might love being hunched over a desk with electronic components spread in front of him, but he'd also been a keen surfer. Bondi Beach had been a favorite place of his to escape to on the weekends.

Needless to say, he didn't get to surf anymore.

Suddenly, there was a loud rushing noise in the sky. Frowning, he glanced up—and saw a small raptor ptero ship whizz by overhead.

Fucking hell. He froze. What were they doing so close to base?

Another flew past. Its shape was so distinctive—

like the flying dinosaurs of Earth's past, it had two large wings, and narrowed into points at both the front and back. Red lights glowed along the wings and what had to be the cockpit window at the front.

Fear spurred him to action, and Noah started to run. He glimpsed the pteros wheeling around, pointed wings aimed at the ground as they executed impossibly tight turns. Apparently, it had been too much to hope that they hadn't seen him.

Shit.

They flew straight back in his direction.

Noah pumped his arms, his heart thumping in his chest. He went to the gym, kept fit. But deep down, he knew he couldn't cross the clearing in time.

Green poison splattered the ground around him. He skidded to a halt, dirt flying, and dodged to the side.

Frantically, he checked he hadn't been hit. Nearby, he heard the sizzle as the raptor poison ate through the grass and dirt. He knew the stuff paralyzed, and apparently hurt like hell. He ran again, pushing for all the speed he had. He glanced back and saw the ships turning again for another pass. *Shit, shit, shit.*

Suddenly, people poured out of the trees. Soldiers dressed in black carbon fiber armor.

"Noah!" Marcus Steele yelled. "Get down."

Noah dropped.

Marcus was leader of the base's roughest, toughest group of commandos—Hell Squad. The rest of Hell Squad's soldiers fanned out. They were all holding their carbines, aiming into the sky. One of them, Reed MacKinnon, held a modified carbine Noah knew could also fire explosives.

And the squad's sniper, Shaw Baird, was balancing a laser-guided missile launcher on his shoulder. The squad's only female soldier, Claudia Frost, stood beside him, her laser scope held up as she targeted the enemy.

"Steady," she said. "Steady. Fire!"

Shaw fired the rocket launcher. The missile launched, Shaw absorbing the recoil. The rest of the squad members were firing their carbines.

Noah couldn't stop himself, he looked back over his shoulder.

The missile flew straight and slammed into the lead ptero.

It exploded in a ball of flames.

Noah held his arm up to shield his face from the huge explosion. The second ptero peeled away and, quick as lightning, disappeared.

Noah released a shaky breath. *Hell.*

"Okay?" Cruz Ramos, Hell Squad's second-in-command stood above Noah offering him a hand.

He took it and got to his feet. "Yeah. Glad you guys arrived when you did."

"We're on base patrol today. Elle saw the damn things zipping in."

Elle was their comms officer. Noah knew she was in the base somewhere, monitoring drone feed and providing her squad with intel.

The rest of the squad strolled forward, their largest, quietest and deadliest soldier, Gabe, bringing up the rear.

"That was closer than we've ever seen them," Marcus said.

"Hell, that was too damn close." Shaw set the missile launcher down.

They all stared at the beautiful blue sky.

"Yeah," Noah answered. He felt a heavy weight settle on his shoulders. He had to get the kinks ironed out of Operation Swift Wind...because right now, if they had to evacuate, they wouldn't make it.

"How's the Swift Wind convoy going?" Marcus asked, as though the man had read Noah's mind.

Noah shrugged. "We have a pretty motley collection of vehicles for the convoy. I've retrofitted all of them with small nuclear reactors, so they have power."

Shaw pulled a face. "Why do I hear a huge *but* in your voice?"

"They'll run, but I can't hide them."

The Hell Squad soldiers were all quiet, their faces grim.

"Can't you put illusion systems on them?" Reed, a former Coalition Navy SEAL, asked.

Noah wished. Illusion systems provided a cloak—messed with a vehicle's signature on raptor scans, blurred it from sight, and used directed sound waves to distort any noise. He shook his head. "I don't have the parts to outfit every vehicle with its own illusion system."

"Shit," mumbled Claudia.

Yeah, because if even one vehicle was visible and they were running from the aliens, one vehicle would be enough for the enemy to pinpoint their location.

Noah rubbed the back of his neck. "I'm working on an illusion system to cover the entire convoy."

"I take it that it would need to be a large system," Marcus said.

"Yes. And right now, I can't power it."

"Not even with a nuclear reactor?" Cruz's voice held a Mexican accent.

"No. It's complicated—"

Shaw leaned close to Claudia. "That means he thinks we're dumb."

Noah shook his head. "A large-scale illusion system seems to cause nuclear reactor instability."

Reed shifted. "What about the alien power cubes?"

Reed's fiancée, Dr. Natalya Vasin, was a brilliant energy scientist who had been helping unravel the mystery of the alien energy cubes they'd liberated from the raptors.

"They don't interface easily with our tech. Natalya's been helping, but while we can activate the cubes, pull them apart, and put them back together, we can't seem to use the cubes to power our stuff reliably."

"Damn," Reed muttered.

Damn was right. Noah felt that crushing weight again. The survival of every man, woman, and child in the base was his responsibility.

And he was failing them. He had to get this right, or people would die.

As he followed the others back to Blue Mountain

Base, those words kept thumping in his head. But once he got back to the comp lab, the massive pile of work waiting for him provided a much-needed distraction. He could think more about the power problem later. For the moment, he rolled up his sleeves and got busy.

Almost got it. Noah leaned over his battered desk, hand holding the tiny comp chip he'd just fixed steady as he inserted it back into the comp. Delicate work, but he'd always had steady hands.

Just as he maneuvered the chip into its slot, an alarm started blaring.

Noah jerked, the chip flew out of his tweezers, hit the floor and skittered under the neighboring desk.

He sucked in a breath, and closed his eyes. *Count to three, Kim.*

Finally, he opened his eyes and pulled his glasses off—he only needed the damn things when his eyes were tired. He stared at the orange light flashing above the door. He'd known the evacuation drill was happening this evening...he'd just lost track of time.

He pushed his chair back, then went looking for his missing chip.

Noah knew the drill was important. If the damned aliens invaded the base, they had to be ready to leave. He just wished they had a protected convoy to leave in.

The comp lab was empty, most of his tech team out fixing various things around the underground base. He reached under the desk, searching for the chip. Yep, this was definitely a far cry from his millionaire existence before the alien invasion.

He thought of his parents again. The last time he'd seen them, they'd fought. He'd been off the rails a little, rolling in money and prestige. Yeah, maybe he'd let it all go to his head.

He'd had a collection of expensive sports cars, a fancy penthouse apartment in the city, and had always been at the latest parties and hottest nightclubs. And after the hell Kalina had put him through, he'd worked his way through a long list of glamorous party girls.

His father had been trying to get him to wake up and focus on what really mattered.

"Well, Dad, your pep talk didn't work, but the alien invasion certainly did the trick." Noah cursed, maneuvering his arm awkwardly until his fingers closed over the chip. Exhaling loudly, he went back to his desk and finally got the chip in place.

He glanced up, and the small glowing cube and bits of alien tech on the corner of his desk snagged his attention. And made his jaw tighten.

The lab door slammed open and Roth Masters— leader of Squad Nine—stood in the doorway.

"Kim, alarm means you evacuate." The man was tall and built big. He had a rugged face and ice-blue eyes, and could look pretty intimidating.

Noah had never let anyone intimidate him. "Got work to do, Roth. It's only a drill."

"Yeah, and everyone needs to have this down pat in case it turns into the real thing."

Noah scowled and waved at the tech on his desk. "If I don't get this work done, there won't be anywhere for people to evacuate to."

Roth blew out a breath and nodded. "Marcus told me you're working on power for the illusion system for the Swift Wind convoy."

"Yeah."

"No luck?"

Luck. There was a concept Noah thought about a lot. He reached back and snagged a couple of his dice off the shelf behind him. One was red with white dots, the other a shiny, metallic silver. He had an entire collection of them—of all shapes, sizes and materials—although it was only a small portion of what he'd owned before. These were all he'd managed to save.

"Not yet." Lady Luck was being pretty stingy with him lately.

Roth's gaze landed on the alien cube. "You trying to use the alien energy cubes?"

"No, Masters, I hadn't thought of that." When the soldier lifted a brow, Noah sighed and sank back in his chair. "Sorry. We're working on it, but it seems like everyone needs something these days."

Yep, everyone wanted a piece of him. Some days it felt like he was back at his tech company, where he had accountants to hassle him with budgets, his management team with some new strategy, and tech geeks who wanted jobs, or for him to endorse their latest invention. Oh, and the people who'd wanted money. Women who'd wanted money. Just like his fucking ex-wife.

Roth grinned. "I could always use more tech to test in the field. Marcus keeps riding me about the fact he never gets any of the good stuff you cook up." The man's grin widened. "I'd like to keep bugging him."

Noah snorted. He knew the rivalry between the squads was all in good fun. "Get in line, Roth. I have comps in the schoolrooms to repair, the Swift Wind convoy to work on, and the ventilation's playing up in sector four." A ping came from Noah's comp. He glanced at the screen and when he saw the message, he rolled his eyes. "Oh, and now Captain Dragon has damn well broken the comp in the prison area...again."

Roth lifted a brow. "Captain Dragon?"

"Bladon." Captain Laura Bladon ran the prison area and interrogation team with a damn iron fist. Every time he had the misfortune to step foot in there, she made his life hell. She lived and breathed her work—one of the few things he found admirable about her. She wanted to beat the aliens, no matter what the cost, and that was great—but damn, she needed to loosen up. "I reckon if she could breathe fire, she would."

Roth's lips twitched. "It would match her hair."

That it would. An image of Laura's vibrant red hair flashed in his eyes. She kept it tightly braided, but even when she was nagging him to get her comp system fixed, he wondered what it would look like left loose and falling around her shoulders.

The alarm that had been shrilly blaring suddenly cut off. The silence was deafening.

"Guess the drill's over," Noah said.

"Yeah." Roth glanced at his watch. "I need to go and debrief on the evac. Next time, can you play nice and at least make it look like you're evacuating?"

"Don't hold your breath."

Roth shook his head. "Avery wants to have a few people over for dinner some time. Squad Nine, Hell Squad, you. I think she and Elle have it in their heads you've been working too hard and need to chill out."

Avery Stillman was a former Coalition Central Intelligence Agent. She'd been rescued from a tank in an alien lab and had helped Roth uncover some secrets about the aliens. And in the process, they'd fallen in love. They'd also recently discovered another secret human enclave, hidden underground not far from Blue Mountain Base. A viable, alternative place for them to go if they were attacked.

And sweet Elle Milton was Noah's friend. Noah liked her a lot, had even briefly considered dipping back into the relationship waters for her...but Elle had only ever had eyes for Marcus. Everyone in base was still shaking their heads over the former socialite and the scarred soldier—beauty and the beast.

"Sounds good," Noah said.

But as Roth left, Noah stared at the man's back. They fit, Roth and Avery. Elle and Marcus. They made each other happy and found their own little piece of heaven in the middle of hell. Noah's hand tightened on the edge of his desk. Hell, before the alien invasion, he hadn't believed in connections like that. But each couple had gotten lucky.

Noah lifted the dice, turning them over in his hands. Luck was a capricious bitch, that was for sure. She blessed some and cursed others.

His comp pinged again, and he saw another more insistent message from Captain Dragon. With a grin, he flicked his screen off. That was one thing he'd learned since the apocalypse—you had to enjoy the small pleasures, wherever you could find them.

Chapter Two

Laura Bladon was on a mission.

She strode through the base tunnels toward the dining room, her long legs rapidly eating up the distance. She wasn't on her way to eat—she didn't have time for that. No, she was trying to track down an arrogant, wayward tech genius who refused to obey the smallest of requests.

She lifted her chin, nodded at a few people who passed by. She had her team working to contain a new species of alien—a giant alien bug that looked somewhat like a dragonfly. Roth Masters, her friend from Squad Nine, had brought it in with his squad. Now her team was trying to contain the thing so the medical team could get samples to analyze. And while trying to do that, their comp system had failed...again.

She sometimes wondered if Noah Kim sabotaged it on purpose just to make her life hell.

She turned a corner into another tunnel, and watched a man, woman and small boy walk past. The boy was beaming up at his mother and father, and the father reached out to ruffle the boy's dark hair. They passed her with a smile.

Laura's throat went tight.

She'd had love like that. Before. She'd been part of a big, rambunctious family, the oldest sibling with a sister and two brothers. Then, two years before the invasion, she'd met Jake. Her lips twisted into a smile. Jake had been a soldier and many of the tough men on the base's squads reminded her of him. He'd been a Coalition Navy SEAL, and she'd been Naval Intelligence. She'd tumbled head-over-boots fast for the sexy soldier who'd sauntered up to her at a bar near the base. After a whirlwind romance, he'd proposed and she'd said yes.

In the midst of juggling their busy military careers and wedding plans, the Gizzida had launched their attack on Earth.

Jake had been on a team sent to fight on the front lines that night. She'd watched them get blown to pieces by raptor ptero ships on live feed to the Intelligence Division at headquarters.

She slowed and waited to feel the soul-wrenching grief and horror.

Instead, she felt nothing.

Her steps faltered. From that moment, after Jake had died and the shiny, happy future she'd imagined was hers had disappeared, she'd gone cold. As the aliens had destroyed the planet, the ice had grown a little thicker each day. As she'd lost friends and colleagues, and finally got word that all her family had died, too, she'd gone numb.

She shook herself. She'd survived. She had work—important work—that was helping to fight the aliens.

Laura straightened her uniform shirt. Unless she was alone in her quarters, she always wore her uniform. She stepped into the busy dining room.

There was a low hubbub of conversation. The long tables were packed with people—soldiers, civilians, families, children. She scanned the room, her gaze settling on a table at the back where Hell Squad usually sat.

She saw them there, smiling and talking. Marcus Steele sat with his arm across the back of the chair of a pretty brunette—Elle Milton. She was laughing so hard she was wiping tears from her eyes. Beside her, the lanky, handsome sniper, Shaw, was gesticulating wildly and telling some dramatic story. Beside him, the tough-looking Claudia Frost had her arms crossed over her chest, shaking her head, but even from across the room, Laura could tell the woman was trying not to laugh. Laura was an expert at reading body language. Part of her intelligence duties was interrogation. The small tells and moves people made could often tell her far more than the words they said. It was good at helping her weed out the truth from the lies.

Across the table, Cruz Ramos—Hell Squad's second-in-command sat with his partner, Santha. She was picking at her food, and Laura guessed the woman's morning sickness had yet to pass. The squad's scariest soldier, Gabe Jackson, sat demolishing what looked like a mountain of food. His partner, Emerson, was missing, because the doctor was with her medical team in the prison area, waiting to take alien samples. Lastly, Reed MacKinnon sat with his fiancée, Natalya, tucked close beside him. The alien-lab survivor was smiling, her face glowing.

How did they do it? How did all of Hell Squad find happiness, things to laugh about, and find the courage to risk loving in the middle of chaos? She stared harder at Natalya. How did she do it? Laura couldn't imagine finding happiness after being cut open by the aliens and having terrible things done to her. Yet, here was Natalya, with love stamped on every inch of her pretty face. Laura guessed Reed was good at keeping a woman happy. She eyed the man's strong features and tough, muscled body. God, he reminded Laura of Jake. Reed had been a Navy SEAL, too.

Again, Laura waited for the pain, but all she felt was a vast emptiness inside.

Then her gaze fell on the man seated at the end of the table, watching the others with a tiny smile.

Her heartbeat jumped. Noah Kim was nothing like the battle-hardened soldiers seated with him. He was taller, leaner, with straight black hair that brushed his shoulders. It gave him a rakish air, and combined with his hawkish face and black eyes that illustrated his South Korean heritage, he looked like a modern-day pirate.

Well, he might look like one, but what he really happened to be was an arrogant, know-it-all who did exactly as he pleased. Oh, he worked hard and was a genius with electronics, she knew that, but his holier-than-thou attitude drove her insane.

At that moment, he turned his head and his dark gaze hit hers. She stiffened, and for a glorious second, her belly filled with a rush of heat.

Laura's hands curled into fists. Why? Why, out of everyone here at base, where she had friends she liked, and colleagues she respected, did this man seem to be the only one who broke through the deadness inside her?

She clamped it down, even as a part of her cried at the loss of sensation. Parts of her were hungry to feel, while other parts of her were terrified by it. Especially because of the man who elicited the feelings.

Laura stomped up to the table. "Hi, everyone." She nodded at Marcus and his team.

"Laura." Marcus kicked out an empty chair. "Join us?"

She shook her head. "Thanks for the offer, but I've got work." Her gaze zeroed in on Noah.

The man leaned back in his chair, looking so incredibly relaxed, she wanted to kick him.

"Is your comp broken?" she asked.

"No."

"So why haven't you answered any of my urgent requests to fix the comp system in the prison area?"

"Haven't got to it yet."

His lazy response made her muscles tense. "I need it fixed, and I want it fixed now."

"Like I tell everyone, get in line, Captain. Everyone in this damn place needs me to fix something, or improve something. I only have two damned hands...and I'm entitled to eat."

ANNA HACKETT

She drew herself up, conscious of Hell Squad's gazes watching them intently.

"Well, we need it fixed now." She lowered her voice. "I have Emerson and the medical team down there, needing to take samples from the alien bug Squad Nine brought in. And we can't get the work done without the comp. Plus, with the comp down, the ventilation is playing up. That means we're all a bit hot and bothered. I have prisoners I'd prefer don't get hot and bothered."

Noah closed his eyes and muttered under his breath.

Laura had always had good hearing. "Did you just call me a pain in the ass?"

He ran his tongue over his teeth. "Hell yeah, Captain Dragon, I did."

Her eyes narrowed. She didn't care that they had an audience. "I warned you last time you called me that name that if you did it again, I would knock your teeth out."

"Whoa." Shaw laughed. "Noah, you have the lovely captain well and truly pissed."

Laura swiveled and skewered the sniper with her gaze.

He held his palms up. "Don't mind me."

She lifted her chin. "I expect to see you down in the prison area in twenty minutes, Kim."

She turned to leave.

"Or what?" he asked in a silky voice.

She looked back at him. "You don't want to find out."

20

***

Laura was sitting at her desk, her top shirt buttons loosened, because it was stifling in her windowless office without the ventilation. An underground base provided excellent protection, but without any air circulating, it got damned uncomfortable.

She heard the office door slam open and Noah Kim stood in her doorway. She glanced at her watch. Twenty-one minutes. She resisted pulling a face. She was certain he'd probably stood outside her door for a full sixty seconds just to vex her.

She waved at the main comp console that all the prison area's systems ran through. "All yours."

He made a noise—part growl, part harrumph—and walked over to the desk near the wall. He sank into the chair and started tapping on the screen. "I don't know how the hell you keep breaking this."

Her spine went stiff. "If you fixed the damn thing properly, it wouldn't keep malfunctioning."

He closed his eyes for a second and she got the impression he was counting. "Believe me, I dislike my visits down here as much as you. If I could get the damn thing working permanently, I would."

She felt a tiny little kick in her chest, then ignored him, and went back to scrawling notes in her notebook, since her comp wasn't cooperating.

He muttered as he worked. She eyed him every now and then, when he didn't know she was looking. The man really was handsome, with his long, straight nose and the sharp blades of his cheekbones. Laura would never, ever admit it, but she really liked his long hair, too. Maybe because she was used to short-haired, military types. Since she'd seen him in the dining room, Noah had tied his hair back with a strip of something, enhancing that pirate look. She stared at the thick, black strands and wondered if they were as silky to touch as they looked. When he paused and snatched a pair of dark-rimmed glasses from his pocket and slipped them on, her stomach tightened. They suited him and were mouth-wateringly sexy.

Clearing her throat, she went back to her notes. She was compiling the latest information they'd gotten from their raptor prisoner. His name was Gaz'da. He'd been here for months, and strangely, she sort of felt like she knew him. She never forgot he was a six-foot-five, dinosaur-like humanoid alien who could crush her with his claws. But after those initial months of belligerent silence, he had given them useful information.

Although she didn't always like thinking about the ways they'd had to extract it. She rubbed her forehead. In a war of survival, sometimes they had to cross boundaries they didn't like. Laura knew she was doing her bit by leading the interrogation team and doing the dirty work no one really wanted to think about. She could shield the rest of the base's residents from having to take those harsh steps.

Her gaze went back to Noah. He was sliding under the desk now to muck around with the wiring. All she could see were long, jeans-clad legs.

She swallowed and let herself look. Why? Why

did this cranky genius spark something inside her when nothing and no one else had done it in the year and a half since the invasion? She'd had a type before—strong, military men. Physically fit men who used their brains and bodies in a fight. Jake had fit that type to a T.

Not that Noah wasn't in shape. She knew he spent time in the gym and sparred with Marcus on occasion. But he had the long, lean body of a runner or a swimmer, not a soldier. Would his stomach have a six pack? Would his arms feel strong around a woman?

Jesus. She jerked her gaze away. Pointless ponderings. She was *never* going there. Never ever. Even if she could admit to a physical craving, in every other respect the man drove her crazy.

Sudden shouts came from outside in the hall. Laura was moving in an instant, a frown on her face.

"What's going on?" Noah materialized beside her, following her out.

"Not sure." But her gut had gone hard. Whatever it was, it wouldn't be good. She strode down the main tunnel, which was lined with cells. Each room had its own one-way mirror that let them look inside.

She heard the commotion—shouts and screams—coming from the cell that held the alien bug.

An inhuman screech echoed through the tunnel.

"Fuck me," Noah murmured.

She jogged down the hall, snatched a long

stunner prod from a rack on the wall, and glanced through the window. She took in the scene in one swift glance.

She slapped her hand to the electronic door lock. It beeped and released.

Inside was chaos.

Medical team members in white lab coats lay flat on the floor, fear on their faces. Two of Laura's team were on their feet, trying to subdue an enraged alien bug that was darting around the room, free of the chains they'd had it in.

One of her team, Katrina, was lying face down on the floor, not moving. And Ben, her top interrogator, was bleeding from what looked like a bite on his arm.

She charged in. When Doc Emerson saw her and started to rise, Laura shook her head. Thankfully, the doctor obeyed and pressed back to the floor.

The bug—a giant dragonfly creature the size of a man—darted down and nipped at another of Laura's team, a slim, Indian man. The alien caught Raj's shirt in its sharp mandibles and pulled him off his feet.

Enough. Laura strode closer, and fired up the prod. The creature tried to fly away, but there really wasn't space for it to go far.

She jabbed with her prod, but the alien dodged. It dropped Raj.

Laura jabbed again, but the bug retreated to the roof, its double set of gold-and-black wings flitting fast.

Dammit. Out of the corner of her eye, she

spotted Noah racing in to drag Raj to the side of the room. Her jaw hardened. She'd have to have words with him about staying out of danger.

She grabbed an overturned chair, and righted it.

"Laura, watch out!" Noah's voice.

She turned...just in time to see the bug arrowing for her, mandibles snapping. She dropped and rolled. She got right back on her feet, then she ran. She pressed one boot to the chair and used it to leap high.

She jammed the prod forward, like she was a knight with a lance, and rammed it into the creature's large abdomen.

The high voltage hit it, and it made that horrible screech again. Then it dropped to the floor with a loud slap. Its body was shaking.

Laura landed beside it. "Ben, get the chains."

"It chewed through them, Captain. Like they were made of candy."

Dammit. She scanned her slightly battered team. She saw Emerson and her techs head over to Katrina's still form and check her over.

"Only thing I can think of is that we use the energy chains."

They only had one set of the energy restraints, but they used an electrical field to contain a prisoner. She looked at Noah. "I need that comp system fixed to use those chains."

His dark gaze was on her face, studying her intently. "On it." He turned and disappeared.

"Get the energy chains and get this thing tied up. Emerson, you still need more samples?"

The doctor shook her head, her blonde hair brushing her chin. "I think we have enough. We'll focus on checking out Katrina here, and then look at the others."

Laura nodded. "Thanks." She stalked back to her office and saw Noah focused on the comp screen.

"I've rigged a temporary fix. It'll let you contain that bug right now, but I need to do more work to get the system repaired once and for all."

"It's of prime importance," she said.

He stood and released a long breath. "Everything goddamned is. I only have two hands."

She stiffened. "Then you need to work faster."

In the next second, he was in front of her, towering over her. She hated that. The fact that Noah made her feel...small.

"I have every damn person in this base wanting something or needing something, and I'm also working to make sure if we have to evacuate, we have something to escape in. I do not need you riding me into the ground, Captain Dragon."

Her blood fired. "Don't call me that."

His eyes darkened. "Captain...Dragon."

For the first time in eighteen long months, Laura's control snapped. She gripped his shirt and swung him around until his back slapped against the concrete wall. "Say it again."

His hand closed around hers. "Dragon. You seem happy to live and breathe your damn work every hour of the day. Hell, I've never seen you at the Friday night parties and rarely at the dining room.

Do you ever take a break? Blow off some steam?"

"No." She hated that her voice sounded the slightest bit unsure.

He pushed her back a step, but kept hold of her hand. "You should. You're taking your major uptightness out on the rest of the world."

"I have work to do. Important work."

"So do I."

She raised a brow. "Oh, and you never snap at people or give them hell?"

He shrugged a shoulder. "I just tell people exactly how it is. I don't have time to play the fucking games most people play. Hell, before the invasion, I'd had too many lessons in seeing through people's bullshit." He cocked his head. "You showing me the real you...Laura?"

She took a small step back. "Yes." Why were those dark eyes looking at her like he could see under her skin?

"You seem to give me an extra-special helping of your fire-breathing attitude. Why is that?"

She lifted her chin. "Arrogant men annoy me."

Noah snorted. "Uptight women annoy me." Something flickered through his eyes. "Although money-grubbing liars bother me more."

She wondered at the fury in his voice. "Well, you don't have to worry about money anymore. No one has it."

"That's the truth." He took a step closer, and when she took an involuntary step backward, his gaze narrowed. "I'm not certain you're being honest with me."

"About what?"

"Something else about me bothers you. What is it?"

She shook her head. "I have no idea what you're talking about." God, now she really was a liar. But she wasn't about to share that her body had decided it liked him—her body liked everything about him just fine.

He took another step, and this time she forced herself to hold her ground. He was lean, but there was muscle in his chest, and she felt the heat of him brush over her skin.

"I have work." She turned and closed the few meters to her desk. She snatched up a pile of papers, not even looking at what they were, just needing something to make her look busy.

Suddenly, she felt his body brush against her back and she stiffened.

"You might be the expert in interrogation, but I can sure as hell tell you're lying to me." He expelled a breath and it brushed over her nape. She suppressed a shiver. "Okay, Laura—"

"Captain Bladon."

"You didn't want Dragon, and I actually think Laura has a pretty ring to it."

A finger flicked at her braid, and, unbelievably, she stiffened even more. If this kept up, she'd have sore muscles tomorrow.

"I'll leave you to your work...Laura." There was laughter in his voice.

Laura closed her eyes and waited until she heard the door close. *Dammit.* The man turned her inside out. She took a deep breath and fought for the numbness she'd been living in for so long. She thought of Jake, wished she had a picture of him. All she had were her memories, and she was afraid that they would fade over time.

And even more importantly, she was desperately afraid to risk letting anyone close again.

Chapter Three

The gloved fist came straight at Noah's face. He tried to dodge, but it clipped his chin, and even the partial blow had the force of a freight train behind it.

He stumbled back but caught himself before he hit the mats. "Jesus. Go easy, Steele."

Across from him, Marcus stood, black boxing gloves on his hands. He slammed his gloves together, but he wasn't ducking or weaving or zigzagging. Nope, in the time Noah had been sparring with the soldier, he'd learned Marcus was a straight shooter. He came at you head on, with no subtlety whatsoever.

"You won't get better if I take it easy on you," Marcus said in his gravelly voice.

Noah was getting better. He was no trained soldier, but he had a few skills, and he was starting to feel reasonably confident that he could protect himself in a fight.

When the world was overrun with enemy aliens, it paid to have some survival skills. Not that any human could win hand-to-hand against the aliens. The raptor soldiers were all over six-and-a-half-feet tall, with dense muscle and thick, scaly skin. And their pets were all vicious, animal-type aliens with sharp teeth and claws. The squads all wore armor that was fitted with light exoskeletons that gave them added strength and speed.

Noah used a sneaky combination to slam a fist into Marcus' side. The big man grunted and swung around. Noah blocked and dodged a few more hits before he took a hard one to the gut.

He bent over. "Marcus, what the hell?"

The tiniest smile tipped Marcus' lips. "What doesn't kill you..."

Noah rubbed his belly. "Makes you spit up blood?"

Marcus snorted. "I owed you, for Elle."

"Elle?"

"Yeah. I know you had a thing for her."

Now it was Noah's turn to snort. "Right. Which I never pursued. The woman has only ever seen you." Noah snuck in on the left. "And she has you wrapped around her elegant little finger."

"Fuck you, Kim." Marcus swung a few more times.

Noah blocked, the powerful blows rattling through his body, making him grit his teeth.

"Really, I'm just trying to take your mind off things and help you de-stress."

"What?" Noah blinked.

"I know you're snowed under and stressed...especially about Swift Wind."

Noah bounced on his feet. "I'll get there. I was used to stress before."

Marcus pulled his gloves off and reached down

for the bottles of water they'd brought with them. Noah had just pulled his own gloves off when Marcus tossed a bottle to him.

Noah drank. "If I didn't have a certain dragon causing me headaches, things would be a bit easier."

Marcus didn't smile, but Noah got the impression the man was amused.

"Then I won't tell you that your dragon just walked in."

Noah gave a mental groan and turned his head. Then the water he was drinking went down the wrong way, and he spluttered.

He'd only ever seen Laura Bladon in her uniform. A crisply pressed uniform that covered her from neck to toe. He figured even wrinkles were intimidated by her. Most of the military personnel in the base, by necessity, had given up wearing uniforms.

But Laura wasn't wearing her uniform now.

She wore black leggings that slicked over long, toned legs and hips with just enough curves to make a man's mouth water. She wore some tiny, electric-blue tank that molded lovingly over full breasts and showed off muscled arms.

That long body made him think of the way she'd taken down that alien bug in the prison cell. She'd had this calm, set look on her face. No fear. No concern. She'd been pure skill and power that had been impossible not to admire.

Right now, her long, red hair—hair that always made him think of a glass of red wine—was pulled back off her face in a high ponytail. The end of it brushed her lower back, and made him wonder just how it would look loose. Would it touch the top of her fine ass? How would it look spread out over pale sheets?

Fuck. Noah felt himself harden and he hurriedly looked away and took another huge sip of water. This was Captain Bladon—*Captain Dragon*—he was ogling. Hell, she drove him crazy, and while he could appreciate her feminine attributes, he wasn't attracted to her.

He looked back at Marcus. The soldier was watching him, then he grunted and put his water down.

"What?" Noah demanded.

"Nothing." Marcus slipped his gloves back on. "You'll have to work it out, just like the rest of us had to." His brow creased. "Although I know two people who are taking their sweet time pulling their heads out of their asses."

Noah yanked his gloves on, with a little more force than necessary. "I don't know what the hell you're going on about, Steele."

Marcus swung and slammed an unforgiving punch to Noah's jaw. "Sure you do. But right now, we're going to fight."

***

Laura finished her seated leg press reps, feeling a pleasant burn in her muscles, and climbed off the machine. She took a quick sip of water and moved over to the rack of free weights. She started her biceps curls and let her gaze drift over to the boxing match taking place on the mats.

Marcus moved like a street brawler. He didn't waste time with stealth, he just hammered his hits home.

And Noah...well, he moved far better and faster than she would have guessed. He was using his speed to combat Marcus' strength, and on top of that, Noah was sneakier, too. She could almost see the thoughts swirling in his head as he calculated his next move, came up with strategies, and then executed them. He was using his strengths—his speed and formidable intelligence. While Marcus wasn't stupid—he was a hell of a planner when it came to his missions—he relied on his strength and took the shortest path.

Laura sensed movement behind her, and suddenly she was flanked.

"Mm-hmm," Camryn McNab drawled to Laura's left. "Nothing I like better than watching two prime specimens of men beating each other up." The Squad Nine soldier was a statuesque glamazon with short, feathered hair and dark, gleaming skin.

"I just like to watch prime specimens." This from Sienna Rossi, a curvy brunette and another Squad Nine member. Her gaze was glued to the fight. "Wish they had their shirts off, though."

A snort to Laura's right. A short, compact female was also watching the fight, although her gaze came back to Laura. Mackenna Carides, second-in-command of Squad Nine, was a force to be reckoned with, regardless of her height. "Sienna, you wish all men walked around with their shirts off."

The brunette sighed. "I sure do."

"I take it Squad Nine isn't out on a mission," Laura said.

Mac shook her head. "Nope. Day off. But we are on call. Theron and Taylor are running a self-defense course for the base's women next door."

Laura's eyes widened. "Oh, I bet Theron loves that." Theron was a tall, silent mountain of a man. He preferred to be on a mission, reading, or drinking a beer with his squad mates. As far as she knew, talking was not high on his list of fun things to do, and Laura knew some of the base's women loved to talk.

Mac smiled. "No, he does not."

"And Roth?" Laura didn't spot Squad Nine's leader anywhere in the gym.

"Oh, please." Cam waved a hand. "That man...if we aren't on a mission or in debrief, he's got Avery holed up in their quarters and they're banging each other's brains out."

Laura fought a smile. Roth and former CCIA agent, Avery, had survived crash-landing on a mission, being taken hostage by rogue humans, and being attacked by aliens. Laura had no idea how the two of them had managed to fall in love in the middle of all that, but they had.

A lump lodged in Laura's throat. Roth was another soldier who reminded her of Jake. He was tall, broad, dedicated to his squad and his job. He was a protector, like Jake had been. She was thrilled he and Avery had found each other, but God, it made her feel so empty at the same time.

She blindly turned back to the mat and her gaze found Noah. He was scowling at Marcus, rubbing his jaw. Then he laughed. His dark hair was pulled back and she got the image of him standing at the helm of a pirate ship, legs braced for the roll of the sea, his intelligent gaze focused on the horizon and whatever treasure he was planning to plunder.

Sienna sighed. "I'd like to be banging someone's brains out."

"Thought you were snuggling up with that schoolteacher," Mac said.

Sienna wrinkled her nose. "Didn't work out. He was a little intimidated, I think."

Cam sighed too. "I'd like sex, too. But no one's taken my fancy."

Laura cleared her throat. She noticed things, things others sometimes missed. "Oh? I thought I noticed you paying great attention to Hemi Rahia."

Cam made a choking sound, and Sienna and Mac turned with wide, interested gazes.

"That Neanderthal from Squad Three?" Cam spluttered. "No. No way in hell."

"When I'm questioning someone and they protest too much..." Laura let it hang.

Cam's dark eyes narrowed and she thrust a hand on her hip. "How about we talk about you watching Mr. Sexy King of the Geeks like he's a hot fudge sundae and you're suffering with a sugar craving, instead?"

Laura's mouth slammed shut. The other women

rounded on her now...but just then, the base sirens started wailing. It wasn't the evacuation alarm, but the signal for the squads.

"Shit." Mac straightened and all signs of teasing vanished from her face. "Got to run. Bye Laura."

The women jogged out, along with several other squad soldiers who'd been working out. Marcus tossed his gloves to the edge of the mat, said something to Noah and strode out the door.

Laura glanced over and realized it was just her and Noah left in the gym.

Great. Just great.

"Captain."

"Kim."

He held up the gloves, and there was the tiniest hint of a smile on his lips. "Wanna spar?" And a huge dose of challenge in his voice.

Her heart started beating. It was best she got nowhere near him. This strange feeling she got every time she was near him would die eventually, especially if she starved it of air.

"No, thanks."

He gave a thoughtful nod. "You're afraid...I get it."

Her spine went stiff. "Afraid? Of you?"

"Yeah. Otherwise I thought you'd jump all over the chance to beat me up."

She strode across the mats. "All right, Kim, you want me to beat you up? Well, bring it on."

***

When Laura slammed her glove into Noah's stomach, the air rushed out of his lungs with an *oomf.*

He jumped back, scowling at her. He'd imagined they would trade a few punches, not that she'd go after him like a prizefighter out to win the title.

"Jesus, you can pack a punch."

"You wanted to fight, right? We're not here to be nice to each other."

He came in with a left hook. She blocked and hit out at him. They circled around, getting in hits where they could. Noah couldn't bring himself to put much power behind his punches. If he hit a girl, his mother would be frowning at him from wherever she was now. But it appeared that Laura didn't feel the same compulsion.

She caught his jaw, turning his head. His teeth clicked together. *Goddammit.* "Why the hell don't you like me?" he spat out.

She bounced on her toes, slapping her gloves together. "I told you, I don't like arrogant men."

Noah made a sound. "I tell the truth, whether people like hearing it or not. If that makes me arrogant, so be it. I don't like uptight, rule-loving women, either. So I guess we're even."

"I'm not uptight."

"Honey, you're strung tighter than Cruz's guitar."

He saw a flush of dull color on her cheekbones. "We're in the middle of an apocalypse. I'm focused on my work."

"So is Marcus, along with the other members of

Hell Squad, and all the other squads. They know when to blow off some steam, find some pleasure when they can."

"I had pleasure. I had love." The words broke out of her like bullets.

Noah froze. *Shit.* He'd hit a nerve. "You lost someone."

"Yes." A harsh whisper.

God, he was an idiot. "I'm sorry."

Laura turned away. "I lost a family I loved. I lost the man I loved." She pressed her gloves to her face. "Dammit, I don't want to talk about this with you."

"Hey." He pushed her gloves down, grateful to see while there was sadness on her face, she wasn't crying. "I lost my family, too. Did you have kids?"

She shook her head. "No. We were engaged. Children were in the plan for the future."

A future that had never come to fruition. He pressed a glove to her shoulder and wished he could comfort her.

"Were you married?" she asked. "Did you have children?"

"No kids, but I was married for a while. And my wife...well, I wish I could say I missed her."

Laura gasped.

Noah dragged in a breath. "Ex-wife. Long, ugly story. But I am sorry you're still grieving over your family and your man."

Her face hardened. "That's just it. I'm not. Most days I don't feel anything." She lifted her hands. "Come on. Are we fighting, or what?"

She came at Noah so fast, his head spun.

He blocked her blows, struggling to keep her from knocking his teeth out. They moved backward across the mat.

"You've been training with Marcus. You must be better than this."

He knew she was taunting him. Knew something hot and ugly was driving her. And dammit, he hated seeing that deliberately blank face that was hiding pain. She might say she didn't feel anything but it was there, buried deep.

He swung out with a good hit. This time she went back a step. Her eyes heated. "That's more like it."

They circled each other and she jumped in close, getting in a punch to his shoulder. She'd dropped her guard, though, and he drove his glove into her side.

This time, she gave him a small smile. And when she launched at him, she had no mercy.

Damn, she was good. If he wasn't starting to ache—both his body and his pride—he would have taken more time to admire her. She wasn't graceful, she had too much no-nonsense power behind her fighting to be pretty. But she was good and damned effective.

Noah took a step back, and realized he was off the mat. A second later, his back slapped against the wall.

He held up his gloves, his chest heaving. "I guess you win."

Laura was breathing heavily, too. "I like winning."

Yeah, he could see that. She liked everything perfect, the way she wanted it. He'd seen the precision with which she ran the prison area. He could see that if she set her mind to something, she liked to win it.

She started pulling off her gloves. "I wouldn't have got in so many hits, if you weren't afraid of fighting a girl."

Noah yanked on the fastenings around his wrists and worked his gloves off. "I wasn't afraid. But I didn't want to hurt you, and my mother would be pissed. She'd probably come back to haunt me or something."

Laura's face softened for a second, then she turned away.

Noah tossed his gloves. "And you didn't fight badly...for a girl."

Laura froze, then turned slowly. "You did not just say that."

He shrugged. The devil in him urged him to taunt her. It was just so easy. "You guys are the weaker sex, right?"

She made an enraged sound and closed the distance between them. She shoved him against the wall. Hard. "You are just trying to piss me off."

He just wanted to see the color come back to her face, see her green eyes shimmer with life. Not that empty, heartbreaking look she'd had on her face a minute ago. "Is it working?"

"Yes. Damn you." She shoved him again, her

face an inch from his. "Why do you get under my skin so easily?"

In that second, everything shifted. Noah felt it, almost as though the ground had moved. The air between them felt charged with electricity. Up close, he could see she had a smattering of the cutest freckles across her nose, and her lashes were so damn long. Funny that such a tough woman had such delicate touches.

"Same goes, honey. I just have to see a message from you bossing me around and my blood boils."

She opened her mouth and he saw her throat working. Her body was pressed close to his, all those compact curves encased in stretchy, form-fitting fabric. His hand itched to touch, to trace down her body and explore.

She made a small inarticulate noise, then she went up on her toes and slammed her mouth to his.

Shock. Instant fire. Desire Noah hadn't even realized he'd been carrying around went up like a match to gasoline.

He wrapped his arms around her, yanked her closer and thrust his tongue into her mouth. Her hands tangled in his hair, and she made a hungry little sound. Noah couldn't believe how good she tasted.

He wasn't sure how it happened, but in the next moment, he had his hands on her, sliding down, cupping the delicious curves of her ass. She jumped up and wrapped her legs around his waist. Noah spun, pinning her between the wall and his body. When his hard cock ground between her legs, she moaned into his mouth.

"Damn, you taste good," he murmured against her lips.

She yanked on his hair, her teeth sinking into his bottom lip. He jerked against her, his cock turning even harder.

"Touch me," she said, her tone urgent.

"I am, honey. I am." Keeping her pinned, his pressed his mouth back to hers and slid one hand down her side. Strength covered by softness. She was one hell of a package. He'd always known she was attractive, but their feud had kept him from realizing just how much.

And how he wanted her.

He reached the waistband of her leggings.

Her hips surged against him. "Yes."

God, she was hot. And hungry. So hungry. He slid his hand inside the front of her leggings, sliding right under the thin silk of her panties. He felt her curls, wondered if they were as red as the hair on her head, then he touched the warm, damp center of her.

"Shit, honey, you're so wet for me." She was soaked through. In the tight confines, he ran his fingers through her plump lips, then moved to find the tiny little nub.

"God, Noah, yes." Her head fell back against the wall. "Yes."

He worked her clit in circles, testing until he found the right pressure. Damn, his cock was rock hard against his boxers. And he was tantalized by the feel of her, the sounds she made, the smell of her arousal. He wanted her spread out naked, so he could part those thighs and lick her, suck her. *Damn.*

"I...I..." she made a choked cry and her eyes locked with his.

"That's it, honey. Just let it come."

Her orgasm hit her hard. He kept working her and she leaned forward, her face slamming into his shoulder. He felt her teeth as she bit him to muffle her scream.

Holy hell. As they stayed there, his hand trapped between her sleek thighs, her juices on his fingers, and her warm body plastered to his, all Noah could think about was sinking his aching cock inside her. "Laura—"

She pulled back like he'd electrocuted her. She blinked, her eyes looking a little wild. Then she pushed against his chest. "Let me down."

His jaw tensed, but then he pulled his hand out of her pants and stepped back.

She looked so damn beautiful. Some strands of vibrant red hair had escaped her tie and curled around her face. She had a light sheen of perspiration on her skin, and her cheeks were flushed.

"Laura, come back to my quarters." Noah couldn't remember wanting a woman quite as much as he did right now.

She swallowed, her gaze dropped, lingered a second on where his erection was tenting his workout shorts, then jerked up. The color leached from her face. "Oh, God."

"Laura—"

She pushed past him, and ran out of the empty gym.

Noah put his hands on his hips and lifted his gaze to the smooth concrete ceiling. Damn. That had not gone well. The sexy part where she'd come on his hand, that had been perfect...but that haunted look on her face as she'd fled...not so much.

Now what the hell was he going to do?

Chapter Four

Laura marched down the tunnel the next morning and kept her head high. She nodded at a few people and said hello. Normal. Everything was normal. She was wearing her uniform, her unruly hair was braided. She, head of the interrogation team, was going to have a quick word with the head of the tech team.

A man who'd had his hand down her pants and given her a soul-shattering orgasm against a wall in a public place.

Her steps faltered and her gut churned. How had everything gotten so out of hand so quickly? She drew in a long breath. She was an adult. She was going to talk with Noah, clear the air, and that would be it. Everything would go right back to normal.

The fact that she'd dreamed of him—him touching her, kissing her, fucking her—was not normal. But she was sure it would pass. The fact that she could still taste him, feel the hard press of his body against hers...well, that would pass, too. Wouldn't it?

She strode onward and reached the comp lab. A sign on the door said *"Shh...genius at work."* It steadied her, that arrogant declaration. She even smiled. As he'd said, he was just being honest, so she guessed she couldn't complain about it.

She fought back the awkward feeling taking up residence in her chest and knocked once before opening the door.

The place was packed with desks topped with comps and benches loaded with bits and pieces of unidentified electronic...things.

And just her luck, the man she'd come to see was in there alone, sitting behind his desk. He was wearing those sexy glasses and his gaze traveled over her. "Good morning, Captain Bladon."

"Hi." God, now that she was here, she wasn't sure what to say. Her practiced speech had fled her mind. She resisted the urge to fidget. "Look, I just wanted to talk about what happened yesterday...you know, to clear the air."

Noah leaned back in his chair. He'd left his black hair loose today. It really suited him. She'd never thought she'd like long hair on a man.

"And just what happened yesterday?" he asked.

Heat filled her cheeks. Great. He wasn't going to make this easy. "You know what happened. I just wanted to apologize. It was a lapse in judgment and it won't happen again."

He didn't say anything, that black gaze boring into her.

Now Laura fidgeted. "So, that's it, I—"

"Laura, what happened in the gym is going to happen again."

She felt a flush run over her skin, warmth

settling in her chest. "No." This man might ignite things in her, make her feel gloriously alive...but she didn't want to feel that. Not again.

"Yes." He stood and circled his desk.

Laura made sure her feet stayed planted. She'd never run from anything in her life, and she hated that she'd run out of the gym last night like a coward. It wasn't going to happen again.

He moved right in front of her, and leaned back, perched on the edge of his battered desk.

He was too close. She felt her breathing hitch. He was wearing cologne, something fresh that made her think of rainstorms and the sea. Desperately, she searched for something to break this crazy conversation. Her gaze fell on the small group of strange cubes on his desk.

"Are those alien energy cubes?" she asked. Okay, her words might have been the tiniest bit rushed, but to everyone else she was sure she sounded normal, in control.

He studied her a bit more before he reached for a cube. "Yeah."

"You're studying them?"

"We've been studying them for weeks. I can't get them to do what I want them to do." He held the cube out to her.

She took it, studying the grooves etched in the side, the deep red glow inside of it. She was curious now. "What do you need it to do?"

"You know about Operation Swift Wind?"

She nodded. General Holmes was working hard to get it all operational.

"Well, I need power, a lot of power, for an illusion system to hide the entire convoy."

She raised a brow. She'd never heard of an illusion system so big. "And these cubes don't give enough power?"

He shook his head, the dark strands of his hair brushing his cheeks. "Oh, they have plenty of power, I just can't interface it with our systems. Natalya's been trying...but nothing." He released a frustrated breath. "We need a solution yesterday, because we all know the damn raptors are coming for us sooner, rather than later."

She looked at the cube again, amazed he could do anything with it. "I'm sure you'll get there."

He nodded, but she saw a flash of strain in his face. The urgency and the enormity of his task, they were weighing on him...and she didn't like to see that. She'd been so wrapped up in his arrogant, seemingly insensitive attitude, she hadn't given much thought to the pressure he was under. She looked around the lab, noting a whiteboard at the back with a whole bunch of repair jobs listed on it. She knew he had a team, but she spotted his name scrawled in a bold, masculine script beside the majority of the jobs.

Laura held the cube out to him. "I should let you get back to your work."

He uncrossed his legs and pressed his palms to the edge of his desk. "You figure the air's clear enough now."

"Yes."

He reached out and jerked her between his legs.

Her heart thumped against her chest, her pulse rate spiking through the roof. A voice in her head yelled at her to step back, to escape. But she stayed where she was, close to him, absorbing his heat.

"Air's not clear, Laura." He reached behind her, and gripped the end of her long braid. He tugged out the tie and with careful fingers, started unraveling the strands.

"Noah—"

"God, I love hearing my name on your lips." He finished with her hair, spreading it over her shoulders. "And this…this is just beautiful." His gaze hit hers, locked there. "Last night, all I could think about as I lay in bed was what this would feel like moving over my bare skin."

Her breath hitched. "We can't do this."

"Why not? Two single, consenting adults. Nothing wrong with that."

That wasn't it. She just knew he was a danger to her—not physically, but to something deep within her. Something that was encased in thick ice she was too afraid to break through. "I can't."

He pulled her closer, his hand coming up to fiddle with the buttons on her shirt. "So neat and tidy, it makes me want to mess you up. See the perfect Captain Bladon go a little wild."

"I am not wild." She'd never been wild.

"Why did you come down here, Laura?"

"To clear the air—"

He pulled her closer, their noses brushing. "Tell me the truth."

"That is the truth!"

"Bullshit. You deal with uncovering the truth for a living. You expect me to believe you don't know you're lying?"

She swallowed. *Oh, God.* "More." The word escaped, unbidden, on a broken whisper.

The hard lines of his face softened. "More of what, honey?"

"More of you. I want more."

His mouth captured hers and she grabbed him, kissing him back. She moaned into his mouth.

God. It was just like in the gym, but better. She gripped his shoulders, her fingers digging into his soft T-shirt and hard muscles. The kiss was a battle, like they were both trying to devour the other.

His mouth slid to her neck, his teeth scraping over her skin, making her shiver against him.

"Honey, you taste good, feel good. I want to see that red hair on my bed as I fuck you. Hell, I want to hold it while you suck my cock."

His raw words should have repelled her. No one had ever talked to her like that. Instead, her panties were drenched.

He sucked on her neck, biting down on the sensitive spot where her neck met her shoulder. She moaned.

"Come back to my quarters, Laura. We can have some fun and fuck each other until this craziness burns out."

His words made her desire stutter. Was that what she wanted? A quick fuck here and there, until they got sick of each other? There was nothing wrong with that, she knew plenty of single people in the base coped with the stress of what had happened by sharing each other's bunks.

But she'd had more once.

And Noah's words made something inside her crack a little, and it hurt.

No, she wasn't going back there. To the pain and heartache.

She swallowed and pulled out of his arms. "Sorry. I...that's not what I want."

His gaze narrowed. Desire made his face look sharper, harder. "What do you mean? You want hearts and rainbows?"

"No. God, no." She didn't want anything. She *didn't.*

"Good, because I fuck, I don't do that bogus relationship crap."

Her gut tightened. "Oh? But you were married once."

He gave a harsh laugh. "Yeah, that's what taught me that love is just one big cosmic lie. It's something companies used to use to sell cards and flowers and chocolates."

Laura shook her head. She'd had love, and while she'd had it, it had been amazing, comforting, passionate, supportive. When she'd lost it, it had been the most horrible day of her life. Noah had clearly been hurt, just as she had, but in a different way. She gave a little, hollow laugh. "I don't want anything, okay? Let's just pretend this—" she waved a hand between them "—never happened."

As she stepped back again, he gripped her arm.

"Hell, no. You think this fire between us is just going to snuff itself out?"

"It'll have to."

"It's too strong for that, Laura. It's already singeing us. The fire's going to grow."

She felt that crack inside her widen. A part of her, the hungry part, was reaching out, wanting to touch him.

"No." She kept her voice firm. "Have a good day, Noah."

She turned and walked to the door. She wasn't running this time. This time it was her choice to walk away and she was in control.

"Laura?"

She hesitated. She really, really wanted to look back. Hell, she wanted to run back to him and take what he was offering.

But she made herself walk out the door and not look back.

***

"Noah, what the hell is wrong with you today?" Elle Milton slammed her comp keyboard down on her desk and turned to scowl at him.

Noah just scowled back. So he was in a bad mood. That wasn't exactly news. "You should be used to dealing with me by now."

"I thought I was, but this is a new level of bad." She came closer, her scowl morphing to concern. "It's the worry about getting the convoy illusion system working, isn't it?"

He barely resisted rolling his eyes. Elle couldn't hold her anger or a grudge for longer than thirty seconds. She was the same with Marcus, stomping her foot about the risks the man took. Marcus defused her by tossing her over his shoulder and heading to their quarters. And what they did there, Noah did *not* want to think about.

Thinking about sex just made him think of Laura.

Fuck. He picked up one of the alien energy cubes he'd dismantled. "I'm fine, Elle. Don't sweat it."

He went back to studying the alien parts for the hundredth time. Yeah, he was stressed about the illusion system, but the current reason for his foul mood was about five-foot-eight, with deep-red hair and green eyes.

He kept replaying that moment right here at his desk. Thinking about where he'd gone wrong. He pressed a closed fist to his forehead. He'd always had a better affinity with machines and comp systems than people. As a child, he'd been far ahead of his classmates and usually in advanced classes with kids much older than him. He'd never been completely socially inept, but he wasn't always great at reading emotions in others. He wasn't particularly good with subtleties, either.

And Laura was hiding a whole bunch of stuff under her pristine façade.

He set the cube down. Maybe she was like Kalina. Kalina had showed Noah one face—a beautiful, caring one—until she'd had his enormous rock on her finger. Then she'd been a first-class bitch who made it very clear she'd married him for his bank account. There hadn't been a genuine bone in that skinny woman's body.

But his gut told him Laura was nothing like Kalina.

Hell. Just stop thinking about her, Kim. He went back to staring at the energy cube with a vengeance.

A slim hand slammed down on the desk.

He looked up into Elle's pretty face, and the surprisingly stubborn look on it.

"Noah, I am used to dealing with hardass, alpha-male soldiers. One arrogant genius is nothing. So spill, what's wrong?"

"Elle, I've got work—"

"No." Her tone was hard. "I'm not letting you avoid this. Something's wrong and I'm your friend." Her tone softened, her blue eyes earnest. "What's wrong?"

"I kissed Laura."

Elle blinked. "Laura?" Then her eyes widened. "Captain Bladon?"

"Yeah." Well, it had been a hell of a lot more than a kiss, but he wasn't going into details with Elle.

"You and Captain Bladon kissed? The woman you've been cursing for months, who you said rides you into the ground, who annoys the hell out of you. Who—"

"Got the point, Elle. Yes, Captain Bladon." He scraped his hands through his hair.

Elle cleared her throat. "Did you like it?"

He raised his gaze.

She must have seen what was blazing inside him because her eyes widened even more. "Right. You liked it. A lot. And Laura?"

He sighed. "She's running from it."

Elle perched on the edge of the desk. "She was married, right? Before."

"Engaged." And that was all Noah knew.

"That's right." Elle nodded. "He was a Navy SEAL, I think."

Hell, of course he was. Some dedicated soldier who would have suited her perfectly. "She hasn't said much, but she lost him and her family."

Elle pressed her hand over Noah's. "We all lost loved ones." Something crossed her face.

Noah knew Elle had heard her parents die at the hands of raptors on the night of the invasion. And while it sounded like they'd been selfish, vapid assholes, and Elle hadn't been really close to them, she'd grieved for them.

"We've all lost, Noah. But now, it's about how we pick ourselves up and move forward. Wallowing in the past doesn't help. The past will always be remembered, and the people we loved will always be special. But I wouldn't trade what I have with Marcus for the comforts of life before. And I wouldn't give him up to insulate myself in case I lose a loved one again."

Noah thought of his failed marriage and the painful lesson his ex-wife had carved on his soul. He was honest enough to admit he hadn't left that behind. It was why he'd told Laura they could just fuck and get it out of their systems. That was all he'd done from the day his divorce was finalized. He hadn't wanted to risk letting a woman close enough to eviscerate and embarrass him again.

Shit, he'd been letting his past drive him. He thought of Laura, and those moments when she'd come alive under his hands, pure desire lighting her up. Desire just for him.

He wanted that.

He really wanted that.

Now he just needed a plan to make it happen.

Chapter Five

When his comp pinged later that afternoon, Noah noticed with surprise that the message was from Laura. He dropped the energy cube he was working on. Damn thing was driving him nuts, anyway. He tapped his comp and opened the message.

Hi, Noah. I know you're working to get that energy cube operational for the illusion system. I was wondering if you'd like to question the raptor prisoner we have in custody. He may be able to help. He's become a lot more cooperative in the last few weeks. Your call. Laura.

Noah sank back in his chair. It was a good idea. But damn, he hadn't expected her to extend this cordial invite to him. He hadn't expected to hear from her at all.

He quickly typed a message back.

Hey there, Captain Dragon. Excellent idea. I'll be down there shortly. Noah.

His comp pinged.

Do NOT call me that ridiculous name.

Soon, he was striding down the tunnels to the prison area, a smile on his face. As he approached the reinforced metal door to the prison, he saw a young, female soldier standing guard outside. She had gorgeous, dark skin and black, curly hair that framed her face.

"Hi." He nodded at her. He'd seen her a few times when he'd come down to repair the comp system.

She smiled. "It's Noah, right?"

"It sure is."

"Comp system down again?"

He shook his head. "Something else I'm working on with Captain Bladon."

The soldier nodded and moved to unlock the door. She paused and looked back, her smile still in place. "I heard you like gaming."

Noah's eyebrows rose. "Yeah, I don't mind it. The tech team has a weekly tournament in a few of the first-person shooter games they managed to bring with them."

"I used to play Masters of War with my brothers, and a few of us played when we were at the Coalition Military Academy." She pushed open the door and smiled at him again. "I thought maybe you and I could have a private gaming session sometime."

Noah might not be good at reading subtle signs, but he got this one loud and clear. And shit, looking at her, he would have taken her up on it a few weeks back. But now he wanted a different woman. "I—"

"I'm sure Mr. Kim would love a gaming session, Maggie."

Laura's sharp voice startled both Noah and the young soldier. She was standing just inside the doorway, watching them.

Noah walked in. "Another time, maybe," he murmured to Maggie.

With a nod, and an embarrassed look on her face, Maggie returned to her guard duty.

"A gamer, I should have known." Laura was looking over his shoulder. Like the bare concrete wall was suddenly fascinating.

Noah shrugged. "I play with a few of my team. I'm not a hardcore gamer like some of them. My old company had a gaming division, so I had to have a working knowledge."

"I prefer to read or draw." She spun and headed off down the tunnel toward the cells. "Come on."

He heard something edgy in her tone, but he couldn't decipher it. With a shake of his head for infuriating, fascinating women, he followed her.

She stopped at one door, her hands clasped behind her back as she looked through a thick window into the cell.

Noah stepped up beside her and looked as well.

The raptor was seated. He was playing with a small tablet, seemingly engrossed.

"You let him on our system?" Noah asked.

"Of course not. The tablet has no connectivity. We just didn't want him bored...that's the worst thing for someone in captivity. We've been helping him learn more English. It was the biggest problem when he first arrived. We had trouble communicating."

"But you have people who have learned the raptor language, right?"

She nodded. "Yes. Elle has been helping, since she has a real gift for it. My people are getting better, but there is still so much we don't know."

Noah released a long breath. "I don't really want to know about them, I just want them to leave." Humanity was fighting back, but it was an uphill slog. Noah knew that. For every few gains, there seemed to be a huge step backward.

"The more we know about them, the more prepared we are to fight them. And to prevent future attacks." Laura cleared her throat. "Ready?"

Noah stared at the raptor. "Sure."

Laura opened the door. "Good afternoon, Gaz'da."

Shit, they knew its name. Noah watched the raptor straighten. He had dark-gray, scaly skin that covered every inch of him. He had no hair, just scales, and those burning red eyes that were unique to all the aliens.

"Cap-tain."

Hearing the raptor speak in English sent a shiver down Noah's spine. It had a harsh, deep voice.

Laura pulled out a chair and gestured for Noah to sit. She sat in the empty chair beside him.

"Gaz'da, this is Noah. He has a few questions to ask about the energy cubes we have."

The raptor's red eyes focused on Noah. It was impossible to read anything in the creature's face, he was just too alien, too different. Noah cleared his throat. "I'm trying to use the cube to power some of our technology."

A look rippled over the alien's face, but again, Noah had no idea what that meant. Was he upset? Angry? Resigned?

"I am...a soldier. Not a—" he said a word in his own language.

The guttural word didn't mean anything to Noah. He looked at Laura.

"The closest approximation we have is scientist," she told him.

"Okay. Well, let me ask my questions and you answer the best you can."

Gaz'da nodded.

Noah used simple terms and words, trying to explain what was going wrong. The raptor responded with a few simple suggestions, but he had no definitive answers.

Frustrated, Noah sagged in his chair. "Thank you."

The raptor stared at him. "But I did not provide the—" he paused, like he was searching for the correct word "—information you seek."

Noah stood. "You tried."

Laura had stood as well. "I'm sorry, Noah. I'd hoped you might get something that could help."

God, he wanted to touch her. He shoved his hands in his pockets. "It was a good idea. I appreciate it."

"Wait."

The raptor's word made them both turn.

"I...cannot help you. But a scien-tist could."

Noah frowned. "A raptor scientist could give me the information I need?"

"Yes."

"Well, unfortunately, I don't have one handy."

"There are some...at a research outpost. In your dry sands...in the center of this country."

"Dry sands," Noah said with a frown.

The raptor shifted in his seat. "Desert. I know the outpost location. Many scientists there, doing work on your wildlife and minerals. Only one raptor patrol."

Noah felt a spurt of excitement. If they could find a raptor scientist with the expertise to help him access and harness the energy cube, powering the illusion system should be a breeze.

"Thanks," Noah said and exited the cell.

Laura closed the door. "What do you think?"

Noah crossed his arms, watching the raptor settle back into using the tablet. "I should ask you that. You've had him here for months. Is he credible?"

"My gut says yes. He resisted at first, but he's slowly come around. The recent information he's given us has paid off."

Noah chewed it over. "I'll have to go to General Holmes and explain the idea. No doubt Hell Squad will want in. But Holmes might not go for it."

"I'll help sell it to him. He's a friend."

"Oh." An ugly burn started in Noah's gut. "How close of a friend?"

She stilled. "Just a friend. Not that it's any of your business."

He wanted to push her against the wall and kiss her until she took those words back. But she was right, it was none of his business. She kept pushing him away, and she had to come to him if they were ever going to see what lay between them.

Noah's jaw worked. "Let's set up a meeting with the general."

She nodded and headed back down the tunnel.

Noah gripped her shoulder, and she looked back at him. "Thanks for this, Laura. It was a great idea and, if it works out, it might save everyone in this base."

A small smile played around her lips. "You're welcome."

***

As Laura entered the conference room in the base's Ops Area, she saw that everyone was there already. General Holmes was talking to Marcus Steele and Roth Masters. Hell Squad was lined up against the back wall, murmuring amongst themselves and looking deadly. Elle was seated at a comp, tapping on the screen. A quick glance showed she was looking at a drone feed of the desert. Noah was standing beside her, looking over her shoulder.

But his head lifted, his gaze moving to Laura's.

Her heart gave that hard, one-two thump it always did when she saw him. She might get used to the impact he had on her system—maybe sometime in the next century. She blew out a breath and wished he didn't look so sexy simply wearing a black shirt over black cargo pants, with his dark hair pulled back at the nape of his neck.

"Laura, you made it." Adam Holmes strode over and grabbed her hand.

"Sorry, last-minute prisoner issue. Nothing to worry about." She thought Adam looked tired. There were small lines bracketing his mouth, and his blue eyes were weary. He was working hard on Operation Swift Wind, driven by his need to keep every man, woman and child in the base safe. But he was pushing himself hard. She knew he kept himself a little distant from the residents. He had to make tough decisions, had to be the one they could blame for certain things, so it left him very alone.

Adam stepped back. "So, you going to share this plan you have?"

She nodded and stepped closer to the large screen on the wall and turned to face everyone. "As you all know, Noah is working on an illusion system to cover the entire Swift Wind convoy. However, with our own technology, we aren't able to power it."

There were nods and a few murmurs.

"He's been trying to use the alien energy cubes as a power source but—"

Noah moved up beside her, so close his shoulder brushed hers. Laura felt a flare of heat inside.

"I can't get it to interface." There was deep frustration in his voice. "Natalya's tried, my team has tried, and I've tried everything I know. Nothing. We're missing something."

Laura looked at him, and he nodded. She picked

up the thread of the conversation. "We questioned our raptor prisoner…but he's a soldier, he doesn't have the technical knowledge we need. However, he suggested we ask a raptor scientist."

More murmurs around the room.

"And where do we find one of those?" Marcus said, his voice like gravel.

"The prisoner has given us the location of a raptor research outpost. It's in the Simpson Desert in the center of the country. I've questioned him about this outpost some more. They wanted somewhere isolated where they could study our wildlife."

Shaw made a rude noise. "Somewhere where no one would be bothered by the screams."

"Maybe." Laura didn't like to think about poor animals being dissected and tortured. "But also because they would only have to leave one raptor patrol to guard it."

Roth nodded, his rugged face thoughtful. "Then they can have the rest of the troops back in heavily populated areas, fighting and collecting up humans."

Laura's stomach hardened. She knew Hell Squad and Roth's squad had rescued many human survivors from alien labs and testing facilities. Horror was acid in her veins. The Gizzida had come to Earth to capture humans and turn them into raptors. A truly horrifying thing.

"Elle, can you bring up the drone images of the coordinates I gave you?"

The woman nodded. "Sure thing."

The screen filled with images of red-orange sand.

"There's not much out here. It's hot and dry and desolate. There's a lot of sand, and it actually is the world's largest sand dune desert."

"I don't see anything that looks like an outpost." This from Hell Squad's Claudia. "You sure the lizard gave you good intel?"

Laura nodded. "Coming up on it now."

And there it was. Two orange-colored domes appeared, nestled between large dunes.

All the soldiers in the room hissed in breaths. They'd destroyed a dome like this only hours from Blue Mountain Base. One where the aliens were turning hundreds of humans into raptors.

"It isn't as big as the Genesis Facility," Marcus noted.

"There are only two small domes," Laura said. "Much smaller than the dome you destroyed in the Hunter Valley. From studying the feed, it looks like one is personal quarters and the other is used for their research. Now, I have a recommendation for the mission. I need to perform the interrogation on site."

"What?" Noah surged forward. "No way. The squads go in and bring back a scientist."

"I questioned Gaz'da some more." She pulled her gaze away from Noah's hot one. "There are some high-value scientists out there."

"Shit," Marcus said.

Roth ran a hand through his hair.

"What?" Noah demanded. Then his face

changed. "Damn. We steal some high-value raptor scientist, bring him here, and they might come after him."

Laura nodded. "It might force their hand, make them invade Blue Mountain Base."

General Holmes gripped the back of one of the chairs around the table. "Okay Laura, you're in. You'll conduct the interrogation on site."

"Wait." Noah stepped forward. "I'm going, too."

"No!" Laura snapped. She felt all the eyes in the room swing her way.

"I'm the only one who knows the technical questions we need to ask," Noah said.

"You can sit with Elle, feed me the questions over the comm."

Noah shook his head. "If the comm goes down, which it often does, then what? A mission wasted, people put at risk for nothing, and still no way to protect the convoy."

Desperation bubbled inside her. She looked at the general. "He's a civilian. He doesn't have the training or capability for a mission like this. And he's too valuable to this base." *To me*, a part of her screamed. Something twisted inside her. "We can't risk having him on the mission."

Noah rounded on her. "I can hold my own, Captain Bladon. I'm not stupid. I actually have the highest IQ in the room. And I can fight."

They stared at each other, like two Old West gunslingers.

She wanted him safe. Not flying into some raptor facility, where anything could happen.

It was Marcus who cleared his throat. "I can vouch for Kim. He's been training with me and he can hold his own."

No. Laura pressed her lips together.

Adam's gaze switched between the two of them. Then he sighed. "Okay, Marcus, this mission will be Hell Squad's. You decide who goes. When do you want to launch?"

Marcus stroked his jaw, staring at the barren desert around the alien domes. "I think it needs to be a night mission. There's nothing around there for miles. Nowhere to hide, limited cover from the dunes."

Roth nodded. "I agree."

"Okay, then," the general said. "Tonight?"

Marcus nodded. "Tonight." His gaze landed on Laura and Noah. "Firing range will be free in two hours. I suggest you two plan to get your asses down there and brush up on using a weapon."

Laura nodded, but Noah spun, shot her a scathing look, and stalked out.

As the others left the room, Claudia stopped beside Laura. "Word of advice. Surefire way to emasculate a guy is to say he isn't capable of defending himself. Men are men. Doesn't matter if they're an alpha soldier or an alpha tech genius, they'll still react the same way."

Left alone in the room, Laura closed her eyes. *Crap.*

Chapter Six

Noah strode down the tunnel. He'd finished collecting everything he needed for the upcoming mission—armor, weapon, mini-tablet. He was as ready as he'd ever be.

He'd not been out on a mission before, but he'd helped from this side. Watched drone feed with the comms officers as the squads had moved in. He'd even filled in as Hell Squad's comms officer a couple of times when Elle had gone into the field.

Hell, he was excited for it. For a chance to fight the aliens up close and personal.

His gaze fell on a door ahead and his jaw tightened. First, he had to have a conversation with a certain captain.

Noah thumped his fist on the door once, then quickly bypassed the electronic lock. The door opened and he stepped into Laura's quarters.

She was standing in the middle of her living area and she spun, anger sparking in her eyes. "You broke in!"

Noah blinked. Some things he'd expected. Her armor was laid out on the bed—with neat precision. Almost everything in the room was tidy, including the hand-built bookshelves on the back wall that were loaded with books lined up like soldiers.

What wasn't neat was Laura, and what she was doing.

She had a white sheet of paper pegged up to some sort of wooden easel. She wore a man's business shirt that fell to mid-thigh and left her long legs deliciously bare. His gaze followed them down. Hell, she had damn good legs. Legs a man could easily imagine wrapped around his hips as he thrust inside her. He jerked his gaze back up to look at the rest of her. She was covered in paint.

In one hand she held a paintbrush, but multicolored streaks of paint decorated her arms and her white shirt—and not all of the paint looked fresh. Even her face had streaks of paint on it. To cap it off, the rich, lustrous red hair he loved was pulled up in a messy bun on top of her head.

"What are you doing here?" she said, her tone wary.

Noah closed the distance. He was looking at the painting now. It was as impressive as the woman. She was using paints in earthy tones—burnt oranges, smoky blues, vibrant green and dull yellow. He wasn't sure if the wild, passionate strokes meant anything, but the more he looked at what he thought was an abstract, passionate splash of paint, the more he saw. The blue ruins of a city, the brilliant sunset on the horizon, the lushness of green, overgrown vegetation.

"This is really good."

She shrugged and set down her paintbrush in a glass of water she had on the coffee table.

"I didn't know you painted."

She shrugged again. "I don't just sit around studying interrogation techniques in my free time." Her voice had a slight edge, then she huffed out a breath. "I don't talk about it. I only started about eight months ago. I'm still learning."

He looked again at the painting. It wasn't a paint by numbers job. It was passionate, it sang with emotion. He saw a stack of canvases leaning against the wall. "Well, it's amazing. Where do you get the paint?"

"I make it. Old Man Hamish from the hydroponic gardens gives me a few plant and vegetable extracts so I can mix up different colors. What paint we have in supplies is for maintenance, or for use in the school. I didn't want to waste the supplies."

No, Laura Bladon was far too sensible for that. And here was the passionate heart of her—a part she kept locked up and hidden—on display.

"It's beautiful, Laura." He reached out and tugged on a strand of red hair before tucking it behind her ear. He'd come here all angry at her, but seeing this...well, it had taken the edge off.

Faint color appeared in her cheeks. "Thanks."

"That still doesn't get you off for that damned stunt you pulled in Ops."

She stiffened. "Stunt?"

His hand curled into a fist. "Not capable? Shouldn't be on the mission?"

Her chin lifted. "You are a civilian, Noah. You haven't been in combat."

"We've all been in combat since the day the aliens attacked."

"I'm military. I may not go on many missions, but I'm trained, I have the mindset."

He gripped her upper arms. "Laura, I've been part of this fight against the aliens for eighteen months. I came straight to the base as soon as I saw the bombs start falling." Noah had calculated the implications straight away. He'd tried to contact his parents first, hell, he'd even tried to get a message to Kalina. But the phones had been down. Instead, he'd jumped in his Porsche and broken the speed limit to get to Blue Mountain Base. He'd done a job here once, had known the base had everything humanity needed to be a safe haven.

General Holmes had welcomed him and his expertise straight away.

And after that...well, those first few months had been hell. Trying to organize things in the chaos, welcoming shell-shocked survivors, helping boost systems to do things they'd never been designed to do.

He'd been too busy to grieve for his parents and his grandmother. He'd just focused on what had to be done and piecing a tech team together from survivors who had the right skills.

"Sure, I may not have been pulling a trigger on a carbine, but I've been a part of the fight." He shook her a little. "We all have to fight in this war. We don't have the luxury of hiding and letting others fight for us."

She was staring at his chest.

Hell, she was so damned gorgeous in just that paint-splattered shirt and messy hair. "Why?" he demanded. "Why'd you try to get me off the mission?"

Now she looked up, and there was so much emotion swimming in her eyes. "I wanted to protect you."

His chest constricted. "Laura—"

"I lost someone once." Her eyes squeezed closed. "I...I don't think I can do it again."

He yanked her to his chest. "Shit, honey." There was a lump in his throat.

She pushed against him. "I'll get paint on your shirt."

"I don't care." He pressed his face against her hair. She smelled like Laura and paint. "Sometimes Lady Luck smiles on us...sends us someone who makes us feel good. Looks after us when we need to do something risky." She'd clearly started being nice to Noah when she'd sent Laura to cross his path.

Laura pulled back and looked up, one brow rising. "You really believe that?"

He pulled a pair of dice from his pocket. "Let's test the theory. Pick one."

She eyed the lime-green one that was slightly translucent, and then the other, a fancy metal one that was intricately carved.

Not surprisingly, she picked the green one. Noah

already knew she didn't go for fancy.

"Nice choice." He tucked the other one away. "Now, I'm going to roll. Even, I leave. Odd, you kiss me."

She was silent for a minute. "Okay."

Noah leaned over and rolled the cube across the coffee table. It made a small clattering noise and stopped...on five.

Laura's eyes narrowed. "It's rigged."

Sure it was. Noah wasn't shy about manipulating luck where he could. "Or I'm just lucky."

He pulled her in close. He felt her chest rise on a ragged breath. Her gaze roamed over his face. "Why the hell do you have to be so attractive?"

"Just kiss me, Laura. Stop thinking so hard." He pulled her in and closed the gap between them.

She made a noise. "Damn you." She cupped his cheeks and yanked his face down to hers.

Noah felt Laura soften against him. A growl escaped his throat and he kissed her deep, cupping the back of her head. Wild, wild heat flared.

But eventually, he found some control and forced himself to pull back. She was one hell of a strong woman, but she was running scared from this. He was a smart man...he had to tread carefully here.

"I don't want to take the risk either," he said.

The color leached from her face, and she tried to pull away.

He held fast. "I never had what you had, I thought I did and I learned it was a lie. So I don't want to take another risk, but I can't stop thinking about you." He set her away, then cupped her cheek, running his thumb down her cheekbone. "We have a mission to get ready for. See you at the landing pads."

Noah made himself walk away. As he walked down the hall, he saw his shirt was coated in paint and smiled. There was passion burning in his captain, and he wanted to help her set it free.

Then he straightened. But for now, he had to focus on doing his bit to keep her and the base safe.

***

Laura grabbed the handhold above her head and held on tight as the Hawk quadcopter took off. The rock walls of the landing tube moved past them as they shot upward.

Around her, Hell Squad lounged like they spent all day on a Hawk just kicking back and relaxing. She guessed they did spend a lot of time on them, and more than that, were used to heading off on dangerous missions. They all sat or stood, each one of them appearing calm, relaxed, and focused.

Noah sat nearby, looking pretty comfortable in armor that fit him like a glove. He had his hair tied back, his face set. He was tapping on a small mini-tablet attached to his wrist.

"Ladies and gentlemen," the pilot called back from the cockpit. "Please settle in for a nice ride to the Simpson Desert. We're expecting good weather and clear skies all the way."

"Can it, Finn," Claudia called back. "You make a crappy flight attendant. Stick to what you know best."

"You wouldn't know what I do best," came the laconic reply from Finn Eriksson. "I'd be happy to show you."

"Heard it all before, flyboy." Claudia leaned back in her chair, a small smile on her face.

"Just fly the damn Hawk, Finn." Shaw was frowning. "And quit jabbering."

The Hawk cleared the base, its rotors turned and then they headed west. Laura leaned down a little to see out of the side window. The sun had not long set, and darkness wreathed the mountains. She caught the glint of moonlight on water, and the endless darkness of trees.

A small quiver of excitement went through her. She liked her job, was good at it. It wasn't pretty work, or easy work, but it was necessary. But there was something about heading out on an active mission, a chance to truly fight back, that felt good. She thought of Jake, knew he must have felt like this on missions. She smiled. He would have been proud of her.

Then her smile slipped. But he would also have been disappointed in her. That she hadn't let go, that she'd held onto her grief and pain so hard she'd let herself go numb. He would never have wanted that for her.

"Okay, listen up." Marcus faced them. He looked intimidating, his armor making his broad shoulders and muscled body look even bigger and tougher "Finn's going to set us down a short distance from the alien domes. We'll move in silently and access the first dome. Elle's identified it as the research dome. Claudia, you're on point. Gabe will be right behind you. Reed, you'll bring up the rear." Marcus caught Shaw's gaze. "You'll stay back, find a vantage point and cover our asses."

Shaw nodded. "Prefer to be going in, but I've got it."

"Yeah, heard how much you like going in," Cruz murmured. "Heard you had a little private party with Tabby from supplies and her blonde friend."

Shaw grinned. "My lips are sealed."

Cruz snorted.

Claudia rolled her eyes. "Wow, two quickies at the same time. Talented."

Shaw's face hardened and he kicked his boot against Claudia's armored leg. "Enough with the quickie stuff. It's not funny anymore."

The female soldier tossed her head back and smiled. "It is to the rest of us. Truth making you a little uncomfortable, Shaw?"

The sniper leaned down, his face an inch from Claudia's. "You keep this up, I'll show you just how long I take in bed with a woman."

"Wow, my second offer since we boarded...and I'm not interested in either." She crossed her arms.

Shaw leaned down and whispered something in her ear. Laura watched a flow of emotions cross Claudia's face before she shoved Shaw away.

"In your dreams, Shaw. Focus on the mission or I'll punch you in the face."

Marcus was pinching the bridge of his nose and Laura got the impression the bickering was normal.

"Cruz, for God's sake, don't encourage them," Marcus growled.

The conversation turned to confirming the movements for the rest of the mission. It was then she saw Hell Squad turn from a group of joking friends to fully-focused soldiers. She knew their deadly reputation and now she was going to see it in action.

Laura fiddled with the pins she'd stuck in her hair to keep it in place. She looked over and saw Noah was watching her. Funny how looking at him made her a whole lot more nervous than going on this mission. When he winked at her, she felt something inside her soften. It was time she decided whether she had the courage to take a risk with him.

But first, they had to survive this mission.

"Okay, domes in view," Finn called back.

"Everyone, get prepped," Marcus said. "Hell Squad, ready to go to hell?"

"Hell yeah," the squad members yelled. "The devil needs an ass-kicking."

Laura's hand tightened on the bar. *Let's do this.*

Chapter Seven

Noah stayed in line, running quickly across the sand to the nearest dome. He had his combat helmet in place and a night-vision lens over his left eye. Everything was bathed in shades of green.

Ahead of him, half of Hell Squad moved, quickly and quietly. Directly behind him was Laura, followed by the rest of the squad. He could see in an instant they all worked like a well-practiced team, moving together as one.

Ahead, the first dome rose up from the desert floor.

He'd seen images of the Genesis Facility that Hell Squad had destroyed. It had been a giant construction made of a continuous, amber-like glass, riddled with black striations. This dome was different. It was smaller and made of individual panes of orange glass fitted together, giving it a mosaic look. A second dome was just visible behind the first. From inside, they glowed with light.

"Marcus, two raptor signatures rounding the first dome." Elle's calm voice came through their earpieces.

"Down," Marcus said.

Everyone dropped, bellies to the sand. Noah's

heart was a loud beat in his head. He waited and watched, and finally spotted the two huge shadows as they came into view. The two raptors were talking quietly to themselves.

"Gabe." Marcus' murmur was barely audible.

Off to Noah's right, the big, silent Gabe pushed to his feet, then melded into the shadows like a ghost.

Noah kept watching. All he saw was a blur of movement in the shadows, and then the two raptors were gone. Damn, Gabe was good.

A moment later, Gabe returned. "I dragged them out into the desert. Won't be found for a while, but if they have regular check-ins, then we don't have much time."

Marcus stood and gestured for the rest of the squad to follow. "Let's do this. Shaw?"

"I'll be waiting. Go interrogate some raptor ass." The sniper slipped away.

The rest of them hurried toward the arched door in the side of the dome. As they neared, Noah noted a raptor version of an electronic lock on it.

The team stopped, their carbines up. Marcus cursed. "Noah, can you get this open?"

"I can try." Noah held up his mini-tablet and got to work. He had their database of raptor words with him, and he'd been working enough with raptor tech to hopefully be able to get past this barrier.

A moment later, the door slid open.

"Nice work." Claudia moved forward and slipped inside.

They all waited a tense few seconds. Then Claudia popped her head back outside. "Clear. But be warned, our comms don't work in here."

Marcus touched his ear. "Elle, we'll make contact once we're out."

"Be safe."

They entered the dome.

Wow. Noah looked up and around. They were in some sort of entry. It was empty, but the walls pulsed with an orange light.

Claudia moved toward the next door, Gabe right behind her. Her low curse came through their earpieces loud and clear. "Another lock."

Noah shouldered forward. "I'm on it."

It didn't take him long. He stepped back with a smile. *Piece of cake.* He caught Laura watching him and he winked.

Claudia moved through the door and the team followed. They moved into a larger room, and everyone gasped.

This room was lined with cages, and inside them were a variety of animals. The screeching of birds and the hissing of snakes added to the cacophony inside. Noah saw larger cages farther in. The aliens had captured kangaroos, wombats, emus—hell, even some camels.

"Noah, move it." Reed nudged him.

Noah shook his head and followed the others. He passed a stack of smaller cages filled with snakes. One reared back, then struck against the bars with a hiss.

They reached the end of the animal room.

Multiple doorways led out. Noah made short work of the lock on the middle door and they made their way through the entry, moving toward the center of the dome.

The next room was what Noah guessed was a lab. There were work benches made of a glossy black surface, and amber glassware lined up in rows on them. The alien version of beakers and test tubes. Some were filled with various colored liquids.

"Chemicals?" Laura suggested.

He looked down at her. "Probably." Noah wondered what the hell the aliens were doing in here.

Suddenly, a door on the other side of the room slid open and a raptor entered. His head was down, staring at something in his hands. When he glanced up, his red eyes widened and he opened his mouth.

Gabe moved so fast he was a blur. He had an arm around the raptor in an instant, dragging him to the ground.

Damn, the man wasn't human. Noah had heard whispers that Gabe had been part of some secret Army project before the invasion. That he could do things no other man could do. Noah believed it.

Gabe dragged the struggling raptor over.

"Claudia, Reed, on the doors. Warn us if anyone comes this way." Marcus kicked out a chair. "Gabe, put him in the chair."

It took Gabe a few seconds to slam the raptor into the chair and use zip ties to secure him.

Marcus looked at Laura. "Laura, you're up."

Laura stopped beside the raptor, and Noah listened to her speak a few words in their language. The guttural words sounded wrong coming from her. The prisoner glanced up at her, his mouth falling open. He responded.

Laura nodded and tapped on her mini-tablet. A modulated computer voice said the next few raptor words. The raptor shook his head violently and Gabe jammed the end of his carbine into the raptor's neck. The alien closed his eyes, then responded.

"He's some sort of biologist," Laura said. "The cubes aren't his area of expertise."

"Could he be lying?" Cruz asked.

She shook her head. "I don't think so. My program detects heart rate and perspiration levels. I think he's telling the truth."

"You're sure it works on aliens?" Marcus said.

"Yes. We've tested it on our raptor prisoners back at base."

Marcus huffed out a breath. "Okay. Gabe, stash him somewhere where he won't be found."

Gabe yanked the alien off the chair and dragged him toward some large metal storage boxes.

"Noah, open the next door," Marcus ordered.

Noah had the hang of the system now and the next door opened in seconds. The next room had long metal tables laid out. The bodies of dead animals, some of them dissected, lay on a few of the tables. Noah gritted his teeth. *Bastards.* Toward the back of the room was a divider made of clouded amber glass. Behind it, they saw a large shadow moving.

They all froze.

Marcus used some hand signals, and this time Claudia crept forward. She peered around, then waved them closer.

When Noah got close enough, he looked around the glass.

A raptor was working, bent over one of the tables. There was a dead kangaroo on the table, cut open, and the raptor was taking samples.

Noah stepped back and shook his head. They needed a raptor scientist who worked with the cubes.

They worked their way through a few more rooms.

Finally, they stepped into a room lined with raptor comp screens. They were made of a black, glass-like substance with ragged edges. Noah had pulled a few apart in the name of research. He followed the line of screens and off to one side, he saw a large pile of stacked energy cubes. From the number of them, he guessed they powered the entire facility.

There was also a raptor working at one of the screens.

Noah nodded.

And Hell Squad moved.

A second later, Claudia and Reed had dragged the raptor off his chair.

"Let's get out of here," Marcus said. "Noah, do your magic."

Noah headed for the door. He held up his tablet and started tapping away. But this time, before he'd cracked the lock, the door clicked and started to open.

Oh, hell. He took a step back.

A huge raptor entered, took one look at Noah, then tackled him to the ground.

Fuck. The landing was hard. Noah's tablet flew out of his hands. The weight of the alien had driven all the air out of his lungs. He kicked out, trying to buck the creature off him. But then the alien clamped scaled hands around Noah's neck.

Shit. Shit. Noah forced himself to relax. Analyze the problem. *Exoskeleton.* He didn't have the strength to battle the raptor, but his armor did. *Follow Marcus' training.* Noah jammed an elbow into the raptor's face and a knee into the alien's side.

The raptor grunted, his hands loosened.

Noah managed to roll and get on top. He slammed a punch at the alien's ugly face.

Then a carbine was aimed into the raptor's temple. A cool, female voice spoke a few words in the language of the aliens.

Noah looked up at Laura. Damn, she looked badass with that hard, take-no-prisoners look on her face.

Beneath him, the alien sagged in defeat. Noah pushed off him. "Thanks."

She inclined her head. Then Cruz and Gabe appeared, pulling the raptor to his feet and binding him.

"Nice moves, Kim," Cruz said.

"Marcus is a tough teacher." Noah scooped up his tablet. It had a crack through the screen. *Dammit.* He thumbed the power button, relieved when it lit up. "Give me a second and we'll get out of here."

He went to work and the door opened. He waved the squad out. They moved, taking their two prisoners with them.

They moved through several more doors before the tablet screen flickered. "No, no."

"What's wrong?" Laura leaned over his shoulder.

"Tablet got damaged when it fell. Must be a loose connection."

"Voices," Gabe said. "Hurry it up."

Noah couldn't hear anything, but he shook the tablet and tried to get it to open the damn door.

"Anything?" Laura asked.

"No. Dammit."

He released a breath.

A calm hand landed on his shoulder. "Noah, as you're so fond of telling us, you're the best at this kind of thing." There was a thread of amusement in Laura's voice. "Fixing broken electronics is something you can do in your sleep."

"Yeah, with my damn tools in my damn lab."

"Oh, so maybe you aren't as good as you've been telling us."

His eyes narrowed. "I know what you're doing, Bladon."

"Every man likes a challenge." The tiniest smile. "Is it working?"

"Give me one of those damn pins you have in your hair."

She retracted her combat helmet. Even with her hair damp from perspiration, she still looked damned gorgeous. She reached up and fished a slim, metal pin from her hair. Noah grabbed it, pried off the back of the tablet and went to work.

"Kim, we need more speed," Marcus growled.

"It'll take however long it takes," he snapped back.

"How long?"

"Two minutes."

"You have one."

"Steele, I'll fix this and get us out. If aliens sneak up on us in the meantime, do what you guys do best." Noah found the problem and fiddled with the wires.

Marcus grumbled under his breath.

Gabe moved almost imperceptibly. "Raptors. Heading this way."

Hell Squad shifted. Reed and Cruz stayed with the prisoners, carbines trained on their heads. The rest of the squad made a line, carbines up and pointed down the corridor behind them.

The tablet screen stabilized. "Yes. Come on, sweetheart." He tapped in his commands. The door lock clicked and the lights stopped blinking. The door opened. "Got it!"

"Go, go," Marcus said.

They charged through.

Noah got them through two more doors, and then they were outside. He took a moment to breathe in the cool desert air. The stars overhead had never looked so beautiful.

"Go." Marcus waved them on. "Head to the preassigned location." Marcus touched his ear. "Elle, we're out and on the move."

Noah ran. He sensed someone beside him and saw Laura keeping pace with him.

Finally, they reached the spot, far enough from the domes to not be spotted. There was a small hillock of rocks that provided cover for what they needed to do. He turned and saw Hell Squad coming. One raptor was jogging, the other refusing, and Gabe and Cruz were dragging him. Claudia followed behind, hiding the trail they'd left in the sand.

"Nice work back there. We couldn't have gotten through the doors without you."

Noah turned his head and looked at Laura. "Thanks. Held my own?"

She smiled. "Yeah. You did."

Marcus strode up. "Okay, Bladon, do your thing."

Laura nodded and even in the darkness, Noah saw that focused look that descended on her face. She studied their two prisoners, both kneeling in the sand.

She pointed at the larger, tougher raptor that had attacked Noah. The one who'd dragged his feet all the way. His face was set in mutinous lines.

She pulled out her tablet and started asking questions. The raptor stared over her shoulder, refusing to talk.

Laura sighed. She leaned down and said something in raptor. The alien stiffened, his determination wavering.

"Marcus, take him away. I don't want him in visual range. I need him to make a few noises that'll convince our other friend here to talk." She reached over and yanked the younger raptor closer. He sprawled at her feet, making grunting noises. He tossed a glance at the other raptor as Gabe dragged him to the other side of the rocks.

"Okay, let's see what it will take to make you tell us what we need." She lowered her voice, to something almost seductive, but there was an edge to it. She started speaking in raptor.

The raptor's throat was working, then he gave her a few halting answers.

Suddenly there was a keening sound from the other side of the rocks. Noah glanced over. What the hell was Gabe doing to the alien?

The young raptor trembled. He spoke again and a friendly smile crossed Laura's face. But there was nothing happy about it. "Okay, Noah, ask your technical questions."

Noah cleared his head and started talking. The tablet translated his words into raptor. The young raptor scientist answered, his shoulders slumping. The translation wasn't perfect and sometimes the raptor was confused. Laura had to intercede a few times, but finally, she nodded and stared at her screen.

She held it out to Noah.

He read through everything the young raptor

had said. "Shit. There are some good ideas here." Yep, he could work with this. Excitement zinged through Noah. "This should work." He looked at Laura and smiled. "I think we got it."

She smiled back.

Suddenly, lights flicked on outside the domes, and loud, guttural shouts could be heard.

"Shit." Marcus said. "We've been busted."

Chapter Eight

"Okay, leave the scientists here," Marcus directed. "Leave them bound, and gag them as well. Let's get back to the Hawk."

Laura jogged through the darkness. Hell Squad was quiet and tense around her. They had a kilometer of sand to cover to reach the Hawk. And the commotion behind them made it clear the raptors were searching for them.

They'd make it. They'd gotten what they needed. She'd done her bit, and Noah had been amazing doing his. It felt...good.

"Marcus." Elle's urgent voice. "I'm picking up a heat signature moving in your direction. It's big and fast. Coming in from the west."

"Close up everyone." Marcus swung his carbine around to aim west.

Laura followed suit and they all stared into the darkness.

"It's not coming from the domes, Ellie?" Cruz asked.

"No. It's long and narrow. I think it must be some sort of alien they have patrolling the area around the domes."

Laura kept searching the shadows. She didn't

see anything. God, what could it be? Canids? But the alien hunting dogs weren't long and narrow. "Could it be that crocodile-type alien you guys saw recently?"

"That came out of the water," Claudia said. "No water around here."

So what was long and narrow and could survive easily in the dry desert sands?

The creature exploded out of the dark with shocking speed. It slammed into Gabe, knocking the large man over.

Laura was speechless for a second, horror sinking into her gut. It was a...snake. A giant, scaled snake with burning red eyes and a ridge of spikes along its back. It coiled up, then struck again, this time knocking Marcus back into Cruz. Carbines fired, but the alien snake didn't seem to care. The laser bounced off its tough hide. It slithered through the sands and curled around Claudia, who kept firing.

Then it tightened its hold.

Claudia cried out, her carbine falling to the ground. Laura stared in dread as she saw the creature tightening its coils around the female soldier.

Suddenly, Noah flew past. He held a knife and started stabbing at the snake. It tightened more and Claudia made a choked noise.

Laura pulled her own knife and ran forward. She slashed at the alien snake, but the blade barely penetrated.

The rest of the squad were back on their feet,

firing carbines or stabbing with their combat knives.

Marcus was near Claudia, trying to get his hands between her and the animal. "Hold the fuck on, Frost. We'll get you out."

Claudia made another choked sound, but couldn't talk.

Suddenly laser shots echoed in the night and green laser blasts slammed with precision into the creature's head. One eye was blown out and the creature loosened its hold, making a hideous hissing sound. Marcus shifted and slammed a boot into the snake's injured face.

It bared giant fangs, but from what Laura could tell, it was like a boa constrictor, and strangled its prey. That probably meant it wasn't venomous. Probably.

Another shot and the snake lost its second eye.

Unable to see, it released its prey and slithered away.

In the distance, Laura could see lights heading in their direction. They'd been spotted. "We have to go."

Marcus was kneeling by Claudia. The woman was lying incredibly still on the sand.

Faint rustling noises coming toward them had everyone turning, their weapons up.

Shaw appeared, his long-range laser rifle in his hand. His face was tense. "She okay?"

Marcus lifted Claudia into his arms. "No. Crush injuries. Let's get back to the Hawk."

Laura ran with Noah. The quadcopter appeared

from the darkness, and Finn was there, pulling the side door open. "Everyone okay?"

Laura shook her head. "Claudia. She got attacked." Laura grabbed Finn's hand and climbed in.

The pilot's gaze went past her. "Shit."

Then Shaw was leaping aboard. He tossed his rifle down and then turned back. Marcus passed Claudia up.

Laura gasped.

In the Hawk's dim interior light, she could see that the woman's armor was dramatically compressed in places. It had crumpled under the pressure of the giant snake. Claudia's eyes were closed, her face pale, and she was taking tiny, shallow breaths.

"Hold on, Frost." Shaw laid her down on the floor and knelt beside her, cradling her head. "We'll get you back to the doc. She'll fix you up as quick as you can say Shaw is the best shot in the world."

Claudia didn't open her eyes or respond.

Shaw looked up at Marcus. "You think she needs nanomeds?"

"Maybe. Cruz? Scan her."

Cruz grabbed a first aid kit off the wall, knelt by Claudia and went to work.

Once everyone was in, Finn slammed the door closed. "Hold on. We have unfriendlies heading this way. We'll take off hard and fast."

"Just how we like it," Cruz said.

It was a weak joke, an attempt to break the thick tension inside the copter. Finn flashed a smile but it didn't reach his eyes. "You got it, Ramos." He headed back into the cockpit.

Noah sat beside Laura. "Strap in." He reached over and clipped her harness in.

"You think she'll be okay?" Laura couldn't look away from the injured woman and the men clustered around her, concern pouring off them.

"She's tough as carbon fiber. She'll make it."

"That thing was horrible."

Noah nodded. "I hate snakes."

"No one likes snakes."

Without warning, the Hawk lifted off, rocketing into the air so fast, Laura's stomach dropped.

"Hell Squad." Elle's voice again. "It appears the raptor ground patrol has anti-aircraft weaponry. They are getting ready to deploy it. Repeat. Anti-aircraft weaponry."

"Fucking brilliant," Marcus muttered. "Roger that. Finn?"

"I heard. Someone man the cannon."

Laura watched as the team, as one, looked at their sniper, who was still cradling Claudia's head in his lap. Her eyes were open now and she was staring up at Shaw. He was murmuring something to her and it looked like whatever he was doing was holding her there.

"Reed?" Marcus ordered.

"Got it."

The lanky SEAL climbed into the autocannon seat on the side of the Hawk.

"Incoming!" Finn suddenly yelled from the cockpit.

The Hawk lurched to the side and Laura slammed into Noah. He put an arm around her.

The autocannon made a loud whining noise as Reed fired back.

The Hawk banked hard to the right. Laura clamped a hand on Noah's thigh and held on. Finn was good, really good, but she hated not knowing exactly what they were up against and what was going to happen next.

"Shit," Finn yelled. "Watch out."

Suddenly the wall beside Laura and Noah was peppered with shots. She lunged back into Noah, staring at the bone-like projectiles that had pierced the metal and protruded a few inches into the copter.

"Dammit," Noah muttered, sliding an arm around her.

"Hang on," Finn called again.

He put them into a dizzying spin, and then they were climbing. Seconds later, the Hawk evened out.

"Clear of the weapons," Finn called back. "Should be a smooth ride the rest of the way...unless we end up with pteros on our tail. Reed, stay on the cannon."

"You bet," Reed responded. "Nice flying, by the way."

The pilot gave a wave from the cockpit. "All in a day's work."

Laura looked back to see Cruz digging around in the medical kit. "How is she?"

"Not good." Chocolate-brown eyes met hers. "She's got bad internal injuries."

"Then give her the nanomeds," Shaw snapped. "Quit wasting time."

Cruz's face tightened, but he nodded. He held up a vial of silver liquid. The nanomeds were tiny medical machines that could move through the body and fix the majority of injuries—heal swelling, cauterize bleeding, stitch things back together, knit bones. "We have to keep a really close eye on her. She's got a lot of injuries and the nanos could go crazy."

And kill her. Nanomeds were notorious for having to be properly monitored. But they were out of options.

Shaw stroked Claudia's black hair off her face. She'd lost consciousness. "Do it."

Cruz jammed the injector into Claudia's arm. A second later, her back bowed. Laura winced in sympathy. She'd never had nanomeds, but she'd heard they could hurt, especially in large doses.

Without looking, Laura grabbed Noah's hand. His fingers entwined with hers.

Watching Claudia fight for her life, watching the men who cared for her worry, made more ice inside Laura melt away.

Hell Squad lived life to the fullest, whether they were fighting the aliens or holding on to their loved ones with everything they had.

***

Noah slicked his wet hair back and tried to focus on the energy cubes on his desk. It was late. The lab was empty, lit only by the lamp on his desk. He'd spent hours holding vigil outside the infirmary with Hell Squad and Laura as they'd waited for news on Claudia.

By the time they'd reached the base, the soldier had been fighting for her life. A thunderstorm had been brewing outside as they'd landed. Noah had decided it matched the mood of Claudia's squad mates.

Doc Emerson had been waiting at the landing pads for them, and had immediately whisked the injured soldier away. It had taken several hours, but the nanomeds had healed Claudia to the point where the doc was comfortable telling them she was going to make it.

Tired and worried, Hell Squad had been visibly relieved.

Marcus had slapped Shaw on the back. "Told you she was too tough to die."

The sniper had nodded, then argued with Emerson until the doctor had allowed him in to sit with Claudia.

Everyone had headed off then, and Noah realized Laura had disappeared. She'd been very quiet after they'd arrived back, lost in her thoughts. He'd considered going to look for her, but he'd fought the urge, taken a quick shower and washed the muck of the mission away, then headed into the lab.

He'd already started implementing the ideas the raptor scientist had given them. It was looking promising. He'd made a little progress, but there was still a lot of work to do. He huffed out a breath. He was tired. He should hit his bunk and start fresh in the morning.

He nabbed a pair of dice off his shelf, running them through his fingers. Usually the familiar ritual soothed him. But tonight, it didn't help. He knew all he'd do in his bed was toss and turn. He couldn't concentrate on his work, he was too wired to sleep.

All he could think about was Laura.

She had to come to him now. He'd tossed the dice on the table. If she didn't want him enough, if she was too afraid to take a chance, there wasn't anything he could do.

He thought of her, in her armor, weapon held with competence, facing down the raptor attacking him. Sexy strength. Courage. Another image followed, of her questioning the aliens—not with brute force, but with that implacable will, and quiet patience. She was unlike anyone he'd ever known.

Fuck. He wasn't going to wait for her to come to him.

He flicked off the light and left the lab. The tunnels were all empty, all off-duty personnel and residents asleep—dreaming dreams of the days before or perhaps nightmares of the invasion. He shoved his hands in his pockets. Maybe a few of them were dreaming of a better future. He sure as hell hoped so.

He reached the door to Laura's quarters. It took him a second to once again bypass the electronic lock.

The lamp beside her bed was on, but the bed was empty, the covers still pulled neatly over it. He glanced around and listened for a moment. Nothing. She wasn't here.

He left her quarters and headed back down the tunnels. Where the hell was she? The horrid image of her sharing someone else's bunk rocketed into his head. He thought of Kalina, and how he'd caught her with her personal trainer. Then he straightened. The past was the past, and he *knew* Laura Bladon. She was honorable to the core. She might be scared of what was between them, but she wouldn't run off to some other guy's bunk in protest.

Noah yanked his tablet out and pulled up the base security system, accessing the security logs. His eyes narrowed. She was outside. She'd taken the southern entrance out about ten minutes before.

Without thinking, he hurried down the tunnel and was soon stepping out of the horizontal tunnel onto the gentle slope of a hill. There were lots of trees, but ahead, there was a small grassy clearing. He saw a bright flash of lightning, followed by the angry rumble of thunder. The storm had reached them.

He'd only taken a few steps when he saw her.

She had her face lifted to the sky, watching nature's fireworks.

She stiffened when he came within a meter of her, and he knew she sensed his presence.

"I was going to wait for you to come to your senses and come to me," he growled against the wind. "But I couldn't wait, *dammit*. I want you and you want me."

She spun. "I don't *want* to want you." There was fury under her words that matched the storm boiling overhead.

It fired Noah's blood. "Same goes, honey. I didn't want an uptight woman who refuses to face the truth."

She stepped closer, her boots bumping his. "And I didn't want an arrogant, egotistical genius. I was happy feeling numb." She yelled the words. Lightning flared, the crack of thunder directly on top of it. "Numb doesn't hurt." She thumped her hands against his chest.

He didn't budge. He was done fighting this.

He grabbed her hands and trapped them against him. The rain started pouring down with a fury that stung against their skin. Australian thunderstorms were rarely gentle things. They were a force of nature.

Just like the emotions swirling inside him for this woman.

He pulled her in close, until his face was an inch from hers. "Stop complicating this. Stop thinking and just feel."

He released one hand and tangled it in her hair. He yanked out the tie and let the long, red waves loose. Then he used the strands to tug her in so her mouth met his.

It had been less than a minute, but the rain had already soaked them through, and the kiss was fueled by the wildness of the storm. He devoured her and she gripped his shirt and kissed him back with the same primal rage.

They battled each other and soon she was wrapped around him, their tongues fighting, hands traveling over each other.

Another flash of lightning lit the sky, and he had the perfect image of her, head tossed back, hair stuck to her skull, passion etched deep on those strong features. The thunder roared—its disapproval or encouragement, Noah wasn't sure.

But he was having this woman. *Mine. Only mine.*

He dragged her down onto the wet ground. They attacked each other, rolling across the grass. They were soaked to the skin, and neither cared. He pulled at her clothes, felt something tear. He had to get to her. Had to claim her.

Finally, he yanked her trousers down and she lifted her hips in a lithe move to help. He left them tangled on her boots and she kicked them free. He slid a hand up a sleek, strong thigh. Damn, she was dazzling. He found soaked panties and gave them a hard yank, leaving them in tatters. It filled him with savage satisfaction. Then he was plunging a finger inside her.

She cried out, and he heard it over the storm.

"My name, damn you." He leaned down and nipped her bottom lip. She jerked and he sank another finger inside her. She was tight. Hot and tight. She'd feel so damn good around his cock.

Her gaze drilled into his, her hips rising and falling with the thrust of his hand. "Noah. Noah, do it, damn you!"

He growled. He pulled his fingers out, enjoyed her disappointed cry. He flicked open his jeans and shoved the sodden denim down.

Then he fell on top of her. She grabbed at him, pulling him closer. It only took him a second, then he thrust into her.

She cried out, her head dropping back. It was like a beacon to him. He leaned down and bit into that slim throat. She jerked against him. Her hand slid over his wet shirt, then he felt nails digging into his ass.

"Move, damn you." Now she reared up and kissed him. She sank her teeth into his bottom lip. Hard enough that he tasted blood. It only enflamed him.

He thrust into her. Again and again. She was making small keening sounds that egged him on. He reached down and angled her hips, saw her eyes widen. He knew his thrusts would be rubbing against her clit. He promised himself that later he'd caress that little nub, lick it, suck it, and watch her come.

But for now, he had to claim her the only way he could.

"God, you're tight." He dropped his head to the side of her neck. "So good, Laura."

"Yes." Her hands tightened on him. "Noah."

He felt her body clamp down on his cock. Another thrust and she was coming. As her body contracted around him, he couldn't hold on. The pleasure was blowing out his threadbare control.

Noah didn't slip over the edge, he was catapulted. His thrusts lost any semblance of rhythm and he hammered home.

Then they were both shouting into the storm as they came.

He lay there, holding onto her for a while. There was another flash of lightning, but this time, the thunder was a distant rumble. Noah turned his head, realizing the storm had passed. The rain had become a light drizzle, kissing their tangled bodies.

Dammit. He'd just taken her on the ground, in the rain.

He pulled back. "Did I hurt you?"

She turned her head and his breath caught. She had a radiant expression on her face, her eyes glowing.

He grinned. "I'll take that as a no." But still, he wanted to show her more, something else.

He wanted to take care of her.

Chapter Nine

Laura let Noah tug her up, reorder their clothes as best he could, then pull her back into the base. They were both drenched, clothes sticking to their skin, and her hair was a tangled, wet mess down her back.

Thankfully, it was really late and with the hour plus Noah's stealth—checking at every tunnel intersection if anyone was ahead—they made it to his quarters without being seen.

"In you go." He gave her a pat on the butt, which turned into an overlong caress.

She tossed him a look over her shoulder.

He grinned and shrugged. "It is a hell of an ass, Laura."

He looked...younger, easier, with that smile on his face. It made her realize just how much stress he'd been carrying around lately. That furious mating outside in the storm might have been a purging of sorts for her, but maybe he'd needed it just as much.

"Come on." He grabbed her hand and tugged her toward the bathroom.

His quarters weren't that different from hers.

Well, except for all the electronic guts of comps everywhere—wires bundled on the coffee table, a sleek comp screen on the desk pushed against the back wall, and beside it bits and pieces he was obviously working on.

He pulled her past an unmade bed and into the tiny bathroom.

His fingers made quick work of the buttons on her shirt, then he flicked open her trousers. When he knelt in front of her, her breath caught. He had that same single-minded look of focus he had when he was working on solving some electronic problem. He pulled off her boots, skimmed her trousers down, and then she was naked.

He looked up at her, his gaze traveling up her naked body. She'd never been one to stress over her looks. She was strong, had some curves in the right places, but she was never going to be a stick-thin model...and she never wanted to be. But the look on his face made her breath catch. Made her feel like the most beautiful woman in the world.

He shot to his feet and turned on the shower. Like most of the quarters in the base, the bathroom only had a shower, small sink and a toilet. She'd heard a few of the larger rooms had bathtubs, but she'd never been one for wallowing around in bubbles. Still the bathrooms were a little tired, with aging tiles, and clouded glass on the shower doors.

"In." He broke her thoughts by pushing her under the spray.

Oh, so good. She groaned and through the glass

saw him pause as he was pulling his shirt over his head.

"Honey, you don't want to make that sound, or you'll find yourself with my cock buried deep inside you again."

Smiling, Laura let the water wash the mud and chill away. "I just love that you and Natalya finally gave us all twenty-four-hour hot water." Then Laura raised her arms over her head and moaned again.

The shower door slammed open, and she finally took a good look at Noah Kim, naked.

"You are not built like a genius computer geek," she said, aware her voice was a little breathless.

He was all sleek lines of muscle and bronze skin. His dark hair was wet around the sharp angles of his face. He closed the door behind him, trapping them together in the small, private space and the warm spray.

"You mean I'm not built like everyone's stereotype of a computer geek."

She tilted her head. "Fair point."

He shrugged, crowding her as he got under the spray. "I was in okay shape before the invasion, but I wasn't as fit as I am now...I was too busy inventing and running a company. There was never enough time to work out. But after the invasion, I realized I needed everything in good condition to help fight this war. Mind and body."

He turned to rinse off his head and unable to help herself, she ran a hand down his strong back.

She'd always thought she had a thing for

bulked-up soldiers. But now...she realized she had a thing for long, lean strength as well.

He made a humming noise and turned. Then he frowned. He gripped her hip, turning her, then he went down on his knees.

"Shit, honey, I'm sorry."

She saw the smudges of bruises on her hips and no doubt she had some on her butt too. Their coming together had been wild and rough...and perfect. She didn't regret a second of it. "I've had worse from training."

He leaned forward and pressed his lips to one bruise under her hipbone.

Her chest hitched. She watched him drop small kisses on her skin, and she had that feeling of being worshipped again. He took his time. Studying each bruise, kissing it.

Each caress fired her blood.

Soon she was panting from the need storming through her system. "Noah."

He looked up, saw her face and smiled. That arrogant, all-knowing smile that had at first driven her mad.

He nudged her back against the wall, then lifted one of her thighs onto his shoulder. The tile was cool between her shoulder blades, and his hand on her leg was hot. She watched him looking at her, and thought she should feel...exposed or something, but she didn't.

He made a humming noise, leaned forward and put his mouth between her legs. *Oh, God.* He licked and sucked, his tongue delving deep into her. She tangled her hands in his hair. Sensation rocketed through her and she wasn't sure she could stay upright. It felt so, so good. And he made it clear he was thoroughly enjoying what he was doing.

He found her clit, circled it, licked it, then he sucked it between his lips.

"Noah!" Laura was teetering on the edge, the pleasure roaring through her in a rush.

"Come on my tongue, Laura. Let me taste you."

The sound of his voice tipped her over the edge. She screamed his name and pulled so hard on his hair, it must have hurt.

When she came back down to Earth, he was smiling at her. He stood and tugged her back under the spray.

Despite the long, very hard cock jutting up toward his belly, he squirted some soap from the dispenser on the wall and set to work rubbing it into her skin.

"Put your hands on the wall." He gently turned her around.

She did, and as his hands skimmed up her body, then slid down, massaging soap into her skin and sides, she let her head drop down and enjoyed all the sensations. The hot spray on her, the scrape of his calluses on her skin. She could tell he was a man who worked with his hands. He kneaded the skin on her sides and she had to bite back a moan. He kept working on her with that single-minded concentration of his.

Then he reached her ass, and he palmed each cheek, kneading again. His hand slipped between, delving down to where she was still sensitive from her orgasm.

His body closed over hers and he nipped her ear. "Are you sore?"

She was. But nothing more than an ache. "Not too sore."

He pressed a kiss to her shoulder and pulled back. She felt his hand on her hip, then the blunt head of his cock brushed between her legs. She swallowed, liquid heat curling in her belly.

"I didn't mention it earlier, but I should have. I have a contraceptive implant."

She licked her lips. "That's good to know. Mine is just about at the end of its useful life."

He rubbed his cock against her. Then he thrust inside.

She made a sound that echoed in the confines of the shower. His hands curled around her hips and then he started thrusting.

"You are so tight around me." He pressed a palm into her lower back, shifting her a little so she felt every hard push of him. "God, Laura, this is a view a man would kill for. I can see my cock splitting you apart, see the way you're wrapped around me."

His words made her gasp, made something hot and tight spark between her legs. She wished she could see it.

"Yeah, you like the words, don't you, honey?" His hand slid up her spine. "They make you wetter."

"Yes," she hissed.

"I'll make love to you in front of a mirror some time, and let you see. But unlike me, who loves the view, I bet you'd like it best if I tell you. Describe every naughty little detail. About how your tight body clasps my cock, how warm and wet you are. And damn, I can still taste your sweet honey on my lips."

She shoved back against him, his words inflaming her.

His thrusts got harder. "I know. I'll take care of you, my captain."

"Harder, damn you."

Now he made a noise, a low groan. His hand slipped around her front, sliding down her stomach and between her legs. When he touched her clit, she jerked hard against him. Then he found his rhythm, between thrusting inside her and moving his finger in a tight circle on her clit.

It didn't take long. Her release had already been on a low simmer deep in her belly. Now it exploded out, flowing over her, making her arch her back.

He leaned down and clamped his mouth on hers in a hard kiss. She shuddered, the pleasure so intense she thought she might pass out.

Then he reared back, his hands clamped hard on her hips and he focused on hammering inside her. Her head fell forward, her hands pressed hard against the tiles. A second later, his fingers bit deep and he thrust into her and held himself there. He roared as he came and Laura smiled.

Then he grabbed her and pulled her to the floor. She sat in his lap, the water falling over both of them as they found their breath.

She leaned her head back against his shoulder. "We might never be able to get up."

"I'll get us to the bed...eventually."

His voice sounded a little husky. She liked that. Liked knowing she made it that way.

Finally, he flicked off the shower and got them both on their feet. He wrapped her in a surprisingly fluffy towel. She scowled at it. "How'd you get such a great towel? Most of them are half worn out."

He finished wrapping another fluffy towel around his waist and winked at her. "I control all the important systems in the base. People like to...give me nice things."

Her eyes narrowed. "Bribe you, you mean."

"Bribe is a harsh word, Captain."

She sidled up to him, sliding her palms up his chest. "And what's the most interesting thing you've been...offered?"

He swallowed. "Baked goods?"

"Really?"

"Nothing nearly as interesting as what I see burning in your eyes right now."

Now she smiled, enjoying the game. "Oh...and if I do what I'm thinking about, what are you going to give me?"

"Extra hot water."

She shook her head. "You already gave us hot water all day and night. Besides, I don't take long showers. Usually."

"Whatever entertainment you want on your comp."

She grabbed his hand and tugged him toward

the bed. "Hmm. You'll have to up the ante, because I'm thinking I've got a hankering to have that long cock of yours in my mouth."

He stumbled and it made her warm inside.

"Shit," he muttered.

"No, thanks," she said with a laugh. She got onto the bed, kneeling there, fiddling with the edge of his towel for a second before she whipped it off. "But I'm sure we'll come up with something." She yanked him onto the bed.

***

Noah lounged in his bed, thinking he could get used to this. He had the sheet pooled in his lap and the remnants of their midnight snack on a plate in the middle of the bed. Across from him, a naked Laura was scribbling furiously on one of his notepads.

She was worrying her lip between her teeth as she sketched.

"You really enjoy your art."

She looked up. Her hair was a snarled, sexy mass falling over her shoulders. Desire was like a punch to the gut. How he could even feel a thing when he'd gorged himself on her, again and again, was beyond him. But right now, she looked like some luscious, sensual nymph out to drag some mortal man back into her world.

"I do. It relaxes me." She scribbled again, paused and frowned, then scribbled some more.

"And you've really only been doing it since the invasion?"

She nodded. "I've always loved looking at art, but I didn't think I had the talent to do it myself."

He remembered those striking paintings in her quarters. "From what I've seen you've got the talent and the passion."

Her eyelids fluttered a little. "Thanks. In the first chaotic days here in the base...I was adrift. I couldn't sit still, I couldn't go outside. I had to do something. I picked up a pad and pencil and started drawing."

Yeah, he understood. Anything to keep you busy enough not to think, to keep the frenzied thoughts at bay. He'd started fixing electronics, something he hadn't done since he was a kid. Running his tech company, he'd been too busy to fiddle with a broken comp or tablet. He'd had employees who'd taken care of stuff like that. Doing that again here at the base had reminded him how much he'd enjoyed it. The simplicity of taking something broken and making it whole and useful again.

Laura shrugged. "Besides, I knew there was a chance I wouldn't survive, so if there was anything I hadn't done that I'd always wanted to try, now was the time." Her pencil stopped. "Ja...my fiancé would have been happy to see it."

"You can say his name, Laura."

She nodded. "Jake. He was a Navy SEAL. He died on the night of the invasion."

"A hero."

"Yes. Yes, he was." She sighed. "There were so

many things I should have done or tried while I had the chance. There are so many things I'd change if I could go back."

"We can't go back," Noah said quietly.

She nodded and leaned over the pad.

Noah realized his words were for himself, as well. The past was gone, and while the future wasn't certain, there was still a lot of hope. Hell, the hope was necessary to survival. He let his gaze take in the beautiful, compelling woman in his bed.

It was time for him to leave the past in the past as well.

"You gonna let me see?" he asked.

"Almost finished." Finally she looked up. She had that cool look on her face that he'd learned meant she was hiding what she really felt. "Here you go." She tipped the pad toward him.

Noah stared at the picture and blinked.

Is that really how she saw him? The picture was definitely him, his modesty preserved by the sheet, but the picture made him think of an arrogant, lazy cat draped out and considering a nap.

"Well?" she prompted. "You don't like it, do you?"

"You're damn good, Laura, but I don't look that...pretty."

Her tense shoulders relaxed and she laughed. "Sorry, but you do."

He scowled. No one had ever called him pretty before, and he was surrounded in the base by big, strong military types... No, he didn't really want to be seen as pretty.

Laura tossed the pad aside and crawled up

toward him. "Let me tell you what I see when I look at you."

"Ah—"

She laughed again, a full out, deep laugh that he'd never heard from her before. He liked it. He wanted to hear it again.

"Sexy." She nipped his ear. "Intelligent." She kissed his jaw. "A handsome, hawkish face." Her mouth moved down to his chest.

God, she was going to kill him.

"Mine."

Noah almost missed the quiet whisper, but as her mouth moved lower, he lost all ability to think.

Chapter Ten

In the Swift Wind storage facility, Noah strode between the parked vehicles, frowning as he mentally checked things off his To-Do list.

Sparks flew into the air as the maintenance teams worked on the last of the new vehicles, cutting out pieces and welding on protective plating.

"Noah?"

He turned and saw one of his tech team members walking toward him, holding a tablet. "Danny? What's the problem?"

"We're working on the comp system for the medical trucks. Can't seem to integrate the medical scanners with the system." The slim man held out his tablet.

Noah looked at it, studied the schematics. "There." He pointed to the problem. "Change that, and try the secondary circuit."

Danny nodded, the stress clearing off his face. "God, I should have seen that. Thanks, mate."

As the man hurried off, Noah crossed his arms and just stared at all the work going on around him. The vehicles were almost ready. That was a minor miracle in itself.

They were running another evac simulation right now, so he knew Blue Mountain's residents were busy running down corridors and trying to get to the exits as fast as they could.

But he still only had the alien cubes partially working.

The intel they'd gleaned had got him part of the way there...but he'd since hit a frustrating brick wall.

He passed the truck loaded with the convoy illusion system on the back of it. The system wasn't huge, didn't even take up the entire vehicle. They'd added laser autocannons to the top and protective plating.

With a scowl, he strode to the corner where his makeshift desk was set up. His papers, a comp and those damn alien cubes were spread across it.

Now he just had to get the damn illusion system powered.

His chair scraped on the concrete and he dropped into it and got to work.

A few times, he got the alien cubes linked to his system and saw them flare to life, glowing a deep red. *Come on, you little beauties.* He read the power output on his comp, his heart kicking into gear.

So much power. More than enough for the illusion system.

Then the power shorted out and died away.

Dammit. He slammed his palms against the table, sending papers flying off the side.

"Looks like you're having a bad evening."

Laura's voice made his head shoot up. And in that second, all his problems eased a little.

She was wearing dark, fitted jeans and a deep-green shirt that looked great with her red hair. But his brain took no time remembering what she looked like with no clothes on. And how those long legs wrapped around his hips.

"You missed dinner." She eased a hip onto his desk and set a takeout box down.

He glanced around and realized the facility was empty. Everyone was gone. He ran a hand through his hair. *Shit.* They'd probably told him they were finished for the day, and he hadn't even noticed. He'd been known to have entire conversations while he was lost in his work that he didn't recall later. The rest of the storage area was in shadows, just the lamp from his desk leaving a small halo of light. "You brought me dinner?"

"I did. Soft tofu stew."

He stared at her. His favorite dish. A Korean dish his grandmother always made. One that wasn't on the menu at base. "How'd you get your hands on *soondubu-jiggae?*"

That mysterious little smile he loved played over her face. "I'm an interrogation expert. I have my ways."

"Thank you." He took the lid off, drew in the delicious scent. "I'm not really hungry, though."

She was watching him with that look of hers.

"Don't try and read me." He shoved his chair back.

"I don't have to work very hard to see you're

frustrated, tired and headed for burnout."

"I still can't get these cubes working properly. I can get them up and running for a minute at best, then they cut out." He let out a harsh breath. "The convoy is ready, but I still can't hide the damn thing."

She stared at him for a second. "Why don't you show me around?"

He wanted to tell her to go and let him work, but dammit, he didn't want her to go. He wavered for a second. He'd felt like this with Kalina, felt this urgent need to be with her, and show off to her.

No. Laura was not Kalina—not in any way, shape or form. And what he felt for her wasn't the same, either.

He stood. "Come on." He grabbed Laura's hand and pulled her into the long rows of vehicles. "We've outfitted vehicles to carry everyone in the base. It won't be the most comfortable way to live for a long period of time, but we'll have everything we need." He pointed. "Medical vehicles."

Laura slowed to look at the large medical truck and the smaller vehicles beside it. "The large one can be used for surgery?"

He nodded. "It's equipped with scanners and all medical supplies. The smaller ones are ambulances, I guess you could say. They can get somewhere quickly, tend to minor injuries, and bring back the severely wounded." They kept walking. "This is the main tech vehicle."

It was a truck as well, but had a long, sleek, black trailer. Noah opened the back doors and waved her in.

"Holy cow." Her mouth dropped open. As they stepped inside, lights flicked on, illuminating the high-tech setup.

Comp screens lined one wall and the other wall had built-in benches for repairs.

"All the storage is filled with tech tools and parts. We can repair equipment in here, plus monitor all the convoy's systems."

She turned slowly, taking it all in. "Incredible."

"There are some bunks that can be pulled out of the wall. But my quarters are at the back." He nodded at a small door.

She opened it and peeked inside.

Noah knew it was nothing fancy. There was no room for fancy on the convoy. Its main purpose was to keep people safe as they escaped.

He had a bunk, his own comp, and a tiny all-in-one bathroom. They'd found the warehouse of a supplier who'd made all-in-one units—shower, toilet and tiny sink usually fitted into planes or ships—and managed to salvage some that were undestroyed. The contained units had top-of-the-line water recycling systems.

"Come on." He grabbed her hand again. "More to show you."

He showed her the supply vehicles. These trucks weren't changed much and were just packed with food supplies, clothes, and medical supplies. Other trucks were the main transport units, outfitted for families, or with dorm-like bunks for the single residents.

Noah answered all her questions, feeling a deep sense of pride in what he and his team had achieved. They were well set up in case they had to evacuate.

Except for that damn illusion system.

"What about the art and historical artifacts I know we have stored in the base?" she asked.

He shook his head. "No room. We can only take what we need."

She nodded. "A shame but it makes sense."

"Holmes has a team hiding a cache of art in places we hope the aliens never find."

Laura spotted the next vehicles and whistled. "Now these are nice." She ran a hand over the hood of a black armored vehicle. The personnel carriers had autocannons mounted on top. "Z6-Hunters. I've read all about them and heard the squads talk about them."

"Yep. These are for the squads to use for convoy security."

"What's the plan for the quadcopters?"

"Finn is working on that with the general." Noah took in the shadowed convoy. "At the first sign of attack, the quadcopters will leave and rendezvous at a prearranged meeting point. We can't afford to lose any of them. They'll meet the convoy and help provide security support once we're mobile."

Laura patted the nearest Hunter, then followed his gaze through the storage facility. "This is really impressive, Noah. You've done excellent work."

He shrugged a shoulder. "There was a team of people working overtime to get the convoy put together. My main problem still isn't solved yet."

"You'll work it out."

"If I can't camouflage the convoy...the raptor pteros will bomb the hell out of it before we can get away."

"Hey." She cupped his cheek. "I know you. You'll work it out."

Her quiet confidence made him relax a fraction. "Come on, I have something else to show you." He dragged her to a bus that had been especially outfitted.

He pulled open a heavy metal door at the back and waved her in.

"What's this?" With a bemused look on her face, she stepped into the bus. Lights clicked on automatically. "Oh."

It had been outfitted with four small cells, cordoned off with reinforced steel mesh to hold even the strongest raptor.

"This is amazing." She strode through, studying the cells, then the work areas toward the front of the bus.

Noah smiled to himself. She was looking at the vehicle like he'd given her a diamond necklace. Hell, he'd showered Kalina in jewels, and she'd never looked like this. "Like it?"

"Love it!" She grinned at him. "It's perfect."

"Hey, I forgot to ask how the evac sim went?" he asked.

Laura turned. "Better. The residents are getting faster."

"But..."

Her lips firmed. "Right now, it's a bit of a game. In a real attack, some will panic." Her face turned grim. "Some won't make it."

More than ever, Noah understood the need to take a chance and grab onto what mattered. It appeared what mattered to him was a strong, dedicated redhead who was still protecting herself from heartache.

But he no longer just wanted her body, he wanted all of her. Including her heart.

His own knocked against his ribs. He'd had it shredded once, and he never wanted to feel like that again. But Laura Bladon was worth it.

Now, he just had to convince her to take the leap with him. Even in the middle of an alien invasion with a possible attack looming.

But he did have a genius IQ. He'd come up with something.

"I really hope we don't get attacked." He looked back at his desk and those damn cubes. "Or, at least not until I can get the damn illusion system working."

"Come on," she said. "Come back to base and get some rest."

"I have work—"

She put her hands on her hips. "You need to eat and rest." A tiny smile flirted around her lips. "I can help you with the resting bit."

He smiled back. "You just want sex."

She laughed. "Maybe. And I have this little fantasy of seeing you naked...wearing only your glasses."

Heat pooled in his gut. "Very naughty, captain."

She shook her head. "It's your fault, you know. I was doing fine without it...but now..."

He grabbed her and gave her a quick kiss. She moaned into his mouth, and suddenly desire was a violent throb in his blood. He pulled back and just looked at her. "How the hell did we end up here?"

She cupped his cheeks, her face turning serious. "I'm not sure. A few days ago, I was pretty sure I found you incredibly annoying."

He nipped her lips again. "Things can change in the blink of an eye."

"Yes. So many things."

Noah let her lead him out of the Swift Wind facility. For a few hours, he would just focus on her, and hope that tomorrow would bring the change he needed to solve the power problem.

***

Laura woke, stretching on the bed. The room was dark, the sheets smelled like Noah and sex, and she was deliciously achy.

The man had spent a long, long time learning exactly how she liked to be touched, kissed and licked. Her legs shifted restlessly at the memory of his head between her thighs.

But there was no long, lean male body in the bed with her now.

Funny how she'd only shared a bed with him for such a short time and she could already miss him.

She rose up on one elbow and spotted him instantly.

He was at his desk, wearing only a pair of jeans and no shirt. The glow of his comp screen cast him in blue light. She heard him muttering to himself.

She sat up and grabbed Noah's shirt off the floor. She slipped it on and wandered over to him.

She ran a hand over his shoulders, then leaned over him. God, he was tense. "What are you doing?"

"Working."

"At three o'clock in the morning?"

"I need to solve this." With a frustrated slash of his arm, he swept everything off his desk—papers, tablet, empty coffee mug.

Ah, here was the volatile temper she knew so well. "Did that help?"

He swiveled his chair and she stepped back.

"Don't use your interrogation psychobabble on me."

She raised a brow. "Psychobabble?"

"I've seen you. You can read a person like an open book, then force them to spill their guts. You make it look so easy, no one even realizes you're doing it." He huffed out a breath. "I'm frustrated and pissed. That's all."

On the corner of his desk, she spotted some of his dice. He needed a distraction. She reached for them.

"Don't touch," he said.

Her hand paused, hovering over the small cubes. "Why?"

"I don't let anyone touch them. My grandmother

bought me my first ones and collecting them became my little obsession."

And he didn't want her to touch them. Laura felt a little sting of pain and curled her fingers into her palm. "Did your grandmother like gambling?"

"No. She believed in luck." He grabbed some of the dice. "Whatever she could do to swing some luck her way, she would." He shook his head and stared at the cubes in his hand for a moment. Then, with his other hand, he grabbed Laura's fingers and spread them out. He set the dice into her palm. They felt cool on her skin. "I couldn't bring my entire collection. I just managed to grab a few, but I'm glad I got some of them. They remind me of her, of family. She would have liked you."

Laura jiggled the dice.

"She hated all the women in my life before."

The pleasant feeling drained out of Laura. "All the women?"

Noah grinned at her. "I was a multi-millionaire, Captain. There were women everywhere."

Laura frowned and tried to pull her hand away from his.

He held on. "Most of them were shallow and superficial, and they were users. They were so pretty that they blinded me for a while."

"And you married one of them," she said quietly.

"To my ever-living regret. She was greedy and a liar. And I was stupid enough to be taken in by...her other charms."

Laura heard the hurt buried beneath his words. "I'm sorry."

He shrugged. "Kalina taught me a valuable lesson."

"To not get too close to anyone?"

He went still, then tilted his head. "I learned to value the truth. To try to see beneath the shell and find the genuine in people."

"Really?" Laura let her skepticism bleed into her voice.

"Okay." He wrinkled his nose. "Maybe I've kept myself from getting in too deep with anyone. Like you do."

She stiffened. "This isn't about me."

"Two of us in the room, Laura. Two of us doing this dance."

She looked away, her heart beating faster. She desperately wanted to change the subject. Stupid to think she could learn more about him, but also stop him from doing the same. She opened her palm and tossed the dice in the air, catching the small cubes. "How about a game?"

He stared at her, like he could see right through her. Could see everything she wanted to keep secret.

She rolled the dice between her fingers and lifted them. "Highest roll wins and the other has to lose a piece of clothing."

"Strip dice?" He glanced at his jeans, then the shirt falling to her mid-thigh. "It'll be a short game."

"Afraid you'll lose, Kim?"

He sat back in his chair, his eyelids hooded. "Honey, either way—you naked or me naked—I win."

She lifted her hand and blew on the dice. "So you're feeling lucky, then?"

He ran a finger along her arm. "I know what you're doing, Laura. We *will* talk..."

She felt all her muscles go tense. Why did she feel this irrational fear trying to choke her?

"...another time," he finished. "Because I am feeling lucky." A slow smile spread over his hawkish face.

She recognized the glint in his dark eyes. *This.* This she could deal with. This easy, straight-forward desire. And it felt good. It made everything else shrink away.

"Roll the dice," he said.

She felt a flicker of excitement. She rolled the dice onto the desk.

"Six." He scooped up the cubes, jiggled them, then rolled. His grin widened. "Ten. Lose the shirt."

Laura undid the buttons, shrugged, and the shirt pooled at her feet.

His gaze slid over her. Her breath hitched.

"You are so damned beautiful." He ran his hands up the side of her legs, his palms just skimming her skin. His touch left a trail of sensation in its wake. "You had it so buttoned up, so hidden, that it took me a while to notice it."

"You were too busy wanting to strangle me."

He tugged her in between his legs. "You wanted to strangle me, too."

"Sometimes. But...mostly you just scared me."

His hands clamped on her hips. "You? Scared of me?"

"Of what you make me feel."

As he dragged her onto his lap, his mouth capturing hers, his hands sliding possessively over her, what she didn't tell him was that she was still afraid.

Afraid that if she fell too far into him, she would never survive it if she lost him.

Chapter Eleven

Noah walked down the tunnel, towing a reluctant Laura behind him. "It'll be fun."

"Hell Squad are your friends, Noah. They won't want me tagging along."

He stopped and pulled her in so she bumped against his chest. "They're good people, Laura. They like you. We'll have a drink, and eat, and talk. Blow off some steam. You haven't been doing enough of that."

She made a small noise. "You and I have been blowing off a hell of a lot of steam. Any more and I won't be able to walk."

He smiled and tapped her nose. Damn, he was falling for her. One hundred percent. Now that he'd stopped fighting it, he was enjoying the freefall. "Come on. Let's see that courage of yours." He turned and thumped on a door.

It swung open and music and smells assailed them. The music was something with Latin undertones and the food smelled mouthwateringly good. Cruz Ramos stood there, in jeans and a T-shirt, a striped kitchen towel in his hands.

"Noah, Laura. Come on in and join the madhouse."

They stepped inside. Santha and Cruz had slightly larger quarters, but with all of Hell Squad packed in there, it made the place seem small. No one seemed to mind.

"I'm making tamales." Cruz smiled at them. "Thankfully Santha's morning sickness has eased, so she can handle the smell."

The woman in question sauntered over. She was tall, with long, black hair, copper-colored skin, and pale green eyes. "Hi Noah. Laura."

Laura nodded and held out a hand. "Nice to see you, Santha."

"How's the bump doing?" Noah asked.

"I have one now." Excitement licked through the woman's voice. "Look." She smoothed her shirt over her tummy.

Noah couldn't see much of a bump on Santha's still-flat belly, but she was clearly excited about it. "Great job."

Santha laughed. "Come on. Grab a homebrew, and a seat if you can find one."

They called out hellos to the others. Marcus was seated on the couch, Elle sitting on the floor, leaning against his legs. Reed was leaning against the wall, one arm around Natalya. Gabe and Emerson were beside them.

Arguing came from the tiny kitchenette. "You overcooked them, you idiot."

"I like them well done," Shaw grumbled. He elbowed the hovering Claudia in the side. "Out of my way, Frost. You're cramping my cooking ability."

Claudia moved, but was frowning at the homemade tortilla chips on the tray. "They're almost fried to a crisp."

"They are perfectly done, crispy tortilla chips." Air whistled through his teeth. "Weren't you making guacamole? You know, because you can't actually cook anything."

Claudia hobbled a little to the kitchen bench and Noah noted her wince. She set to work mixing a bowl of green, goopy-looking stuff.

A second later, Shaw was there, sliding a stool toward her. "Sit."

"I'm fine—"

"I can see that hip is hurting. Don't be a stubborn mule."

She sat with a huff and finally noticed Noah and Laura. "God save me from bossy men. Especially ones with nurse delusions."

"Hey, Claudia, Shaw." Noah ran his gaze over Claudia. "Still hurting?"

"Doc fixed everything up, just a little problem with my hip. Has to heal the old-fashioned way. I keep telling Baird here to quit worrying—"

"Not worried. You're too stubborn to be injured long." He dumped his homemade chips into a bowl and nudged them across the bench.

Noah snagged one. "They are a bit overdone."

Claudia grinned and tipped her head back at Shaw. "Told you."

He pressed a palm to her smug face. "I like them well done. You guys can cook next time." He looked at Noah. "How's that illusion system coming along?"

Noah heard Laura make a sound and shake her head. He gave a rueful smile. "According to Laura, I've been obsessed, moody and frustrated."

"Not working out, then," Shaw said.

"Not yet. But I will get there. The info from the alien scientist helped. I'm close…"

Claudia patted his arm. "You'll get it, Noah. You've solved every problem we've ever thrown at you. That genius brain of yours won't rest until you crack it."

"That's the problem." Laura sipped her beer. "He won't rest. He'll collapse from exhaustion if he isn't careful."

Claudia eyed her and dipped a chip into the guacamole. "I think you'll keep him in line."

"This a private party?" Devlin Gray sauntered up.

Noah liked Dev a lot. The guy was part of Santha's recon team, and he was very good at getting into places without the aliens spotting him. He was wearing dark slacks and a blue shirt that wouldn't have looked out of place in a boardroom or a fancy club. The man just exuded a suaveness that you either had or you didn't. And with his British accent, Noah knew the base's single ladies were torn between macho soldiers or a bit of charm.

"Hey, Dev," Noah said.

"Noah. Hi, Laura."

"How are you, Devlin?"

"Good." He took a chip and somehow looked

elegant eating it. "Busy. Aliens are back out in full force." His face turned serious, his gaze intense. "And they're moving this way. Not an all-out offensive, but something's up. Not sure what yet."

Noah's gut rolled. *Dammit.* He shouldn't be here relaxing. He should be working on that damn illusion system.

But just then, Laura's hand pressed against his, their fingers twining. He drew in a breath. Later.

After dinner, Noah stood against one wall, sipping his drink and watching young Bryony dancing with Laura, Santha, Elle and Natalya. Cruz was strumming his guitar, lost in the music. Damn, the guy was good. The women were laughing, enjoying the moment. Only Emerson wasn't dancing, instead staying close to Gabe's side.

Bryony was an alien lab survivor. Cruz and Santha had rescued her and then adopted the young girl. They'd knocked through a wall and her room adjoined their quarters. The aliens had shaved the girl's head, run tests on her brain. But since her rescue, her hair had grown into a cute style that made her look like a little pixie. She was holding Santha's hands, laughing.

Noah's beer curdled in his gut. This girl deserved to live. Santha and her baby deserved a chance. And as the men nearby discussed the aliens and a possible impending attack on Blue Mountain Base, Noah felt that damned incessant pressure again. He looked at Laura, glad to see her enjoying herself as she moved to the music. Not surprisingly, she danced well, loose and limber.

He wanted her to live, too.

He was falling in love with her.

"So, you've taken the plunge."

Marcus' gravelly voice made Noah jerk and spill some beer on his shirt. He cursed and dabbed at it. "What?"

Marcus lifted his bottle toward Laura. "You and the competent captain."

Noah relaxed. "Yeah. It blindsided me, too. I think we were fighting each other because we both knew this was where we were headed. We were fighting to..." he tried to find the right words.

"To protect yourselves."

Noah turned his head. "What's a badass soldier like you know about it?" He couldn't imagine Marcus Steele was afraid of anything. Noah pictured the tough soldier just plowing through anything that got in the way of what he wanted.

Marcus sipped his beer. "Well, I'm not gonna stand here and discuss feelings with you. But I fought what I felt for Elle for a long time. And I see others here ignoring what they really want for all kinds of fucked-up reasons. But at the end of the day, it all comes back to protecting ourselves, doesn't it? Hell, caring for anyone, especially in this messed up world, is a hell of a risk."

Noah blinked. "I think that's the most I've ever heard you say all at once."

"Screw you, Kim." The man's small smile took the sting out of his words.

"But pretty wise words for a grunt."

"Want me to punch you?"

"No." Noah looked at Laura. "It's worth it, isn't it?"

"Hell yeah." Marcus' green gaze fell on Elle. "Every second. Every little thing makes it worthwhile."

Elle caught Marcus' smile and came over. "Come dance with me."

"Hell, no. Don't dance, you know that."

Elle pouted.

Marcus heaved out a breath and pulled her into his arms. "Not standing out there amongst the gaggle. You move, I'll hold you. Right here."

"Fine." Elle sank into him, swaying her hips.

Noah smiled at them and then saw Laura watching. Hell, he didn't dance either. But when she held out a hand to him, he couldn't resist her.

He tugged her in close. "I can't dance."

"Just sway with me." She rested her head on his shoulder. "Most people try too hard when they dance. It was a lesson I learned when I started painting. If you try too hard, you end up feeling awkward and out of sync. Just listen to the music, hold me, and stop thinking about it too much."

He did, pressing his face against her hair and breathing in the scent of her. Her words echoed in his head and suddenly he went stiff.

She pulled back "What's wrong?"

"Shit, Laura, what you just said...it gave me an idea about the alien cubes."

She frowned. "What?"

Adrenaline surged through him. Hell, he should

have tried something like this long ago. "I've been trying too hard. Forcing the cubes into our systems. I need to put them together and let them blend, to find a way to work together. Not force the alien tech to conform to our systems." He kissed her. "I have to—"

She patted his arms. "I can see that. Go."

He hesitated. "You'll be okay?"

"Yes. You were right, I'm having a good time. And if I come back with you now, you'll be so lost in your work, you won't even know I'm there."

He already felt the call of it. A solution shimmering just out of reach, a problem begging to be solved. "Are you okay with that?"

She kissed him again. "It's you. The way you work. I admire it."

Shit, he was definitely falling in love. "I'll see you soon."

She made a shooing motion. "Go."

He leaned in, his mouth brushing her ear. "We'll play strip dice again, right before bedtime."

"Did I mention I'm not wearing any underwear under this dress?"

He choked. "Hell, maybe you should come back with me now."

She smiled. "Go. It'll give you some incentive to get your work finished. Fast."

And she was right. As Noah shouted goodbyes and hurried to the comp lab, for the first time in a long time, the thoughts of his project were entwined with the thoughts of the woman he wanted to claim as his.

***

After a few hours in the prison cells working with Gaz'da, Laura was headed out to the Swift Wind facility.

Noah had spent most of the night working in the comp lab. After leaving the party, she'd visited him, but he'd barely noticed she was there. He was onto the solution he'd been searching for, and his preliminary tests had him fired up. She was glad. The problem had been eating at him.

But he hadn't come to bed, so he'd been up all night, and now he was with his tech team, ready to do a full test of the illusion system.

She stepped out of a tunnel and into the morning light. She waited for her eyes to adjust and breathed in the fresh air. If they had to leave here, it would hurt. Blue Mountain Base had become home.

But they would do what they had to in order to survive. To keep fighting.

And she'd learned from Noah that in order to survive, she had to learn to let go, relax and enjoy the downtime when they had it. She'd really enjoyed hanging out with Hell Squad. They'd clearly learned what they needed to do in order to get up every day, pick up their carbines and go out and fight. Having their partners, their lovers, the people they cared for...it gave them something to fight for.

She followed the path down to the hidden door into the Swift Wind facility. Moments later, she was heading down a set of steps.

She heard voices and the clang of tools. When she stepped into the underground storage area, she saw Noah standing on top of the illusion system vehicle. It was a small flatbed truck with a dual cab at the front and the illusion system taking up most of the back. He was calling down to someone.

She watched him for a moment. This was the man who'd brought her back to life, dug under her skin, and changed her completely.

A swift wave of panic seized her. It didn't mean she still wasn't terrified. She'd loved Jake. They'd had a wonderful relationship and would have had a happy marriage.

But now, she had a second chance. With Noah, the relationship was different; not as easy, but maybe more passionate. They pushed at each other and she hoped that would help them make each other better people. She felt like Noah was her port in the storm, and she could be the same for him.

Because right now, she felt like they were all in the eye of a storm, and the worst was yet to come in this war.

"Hey," she called out.

Noah swiveled. Lines were etched on his face. Tiredness, concentration, intensity. "Hi. Perfect timing, Captain. We're about to test the system."

She nodded. "Well done. I'll stand back here."

She moved back to the wall, and moments later was joined by General Holmes.

"Adam," she said quietly. The man looked more tired than Noah. "How are you?"

"Good, thanks."

"Remember my offer to talk is always there."

Adam turned to look at her. He had a handsome face, and age was only refining it in a way that made him more attractive. They'd formed a solid friendship over the last eighteen months. A few months ago, if she'd had to pick a man she'd thought suited her, it would have been the clean-cut general, not a moody tech genius.

But Adam needed someone who'd shake him up a little. He was slowly bowing under the stresses of leadership. As far as she could tell, he had only two modes: if he wasn't sleeping, he was working to help the base and its residents.

"I'm fine, Laura. We get this illusion system operational, then I'll breathe a small sigh of relief. At least then Operation Swift Wind will be complete. We'll have a back-up plan...just in case."

"Turn it on, Danny," Noah called out, his voice echoing in the confines of the room.

Laura held her breath and clutched her hands together.

There was a hum of something being fired up. She couldn't see the alien cubes anywhere, but she knew they had to be here, somewhere.

The air shimmered with power and then, all the convoy vehicles in the room blurred and disappeared.

A cheer went up.

Noah had disappeared too, but a second later he walked out of the illusion. He slapped his team members on the back. Then he headed toward her and the general.

"Holmes." He nodded at Adam. Then, without warning, he grabbed Laura and swung her into his arms.

She gasped, but then his hungry mouth was on hers. She had no choice but to grab him and hold on.

When he pulled back, he was grinning.

"You did it," she said. "Well done."

Suddenly, one of the tech team called out. "Something's wrong...power readings are off the charts! There's an overload—"

Noah scowled. "What?" He started back toward the illusion vehicle.

Suddenly, sparks exploded from the illusion system. The lights in the room dimmed and the illusion system cut off, the vehicles reappearing into view.

Smoke started pouring out the top of the illusion system.

"No!" Noah sprinted over.

Laura felt like her chest was full of cement. She watched Noah and his team frantically crawling over the vehicle, using fire extinguishers to put out the burning components. Then she heard Noah's string of curses.

"Damn," Adam murmured.

Noah appeared, his face grim. Laura wanted to smooth those lines away and tell him it would be okay.

"Whole system is fried." The words came out harsh, like bullets. "It'll take months to fix it."

Then he turned and strode out of the room without even looking at Laura.

She closed her eyes. This was not good.

Chapter Twelve

Noah stood on the roof, watching the distant horizon. A storm was brewing. A nasty, heaving thunderstorm with big, black clouds and lightning. It would hit hard and fast, then burn itself out.

He kicked the ground. The roof panels here had been made to look like rock. His mind was turning over—alternating between the disaster of what had happened during the test, and seeing all that tech destroyed.

Parts were gone, fried, and they couldn't be replaced easily. It would take him a long time to fix the system and get it anywhere near operational. He looked at the storm again. And that was time he didn't have.

"Noah?"

He'd been so lost in his dark thoughts, he hadn't heard her. "I'm not good company right now."

She moved beside him. "I don't mind." A moment of charged silence. "What can I do to help?"

"Nothing." He pressed his hands to the back of his head, then swung them down by his sides, restless energy rampaging through him. "I have to start from scratch. You heard Devlin at the party, the aliens are coming this way. Maybe not today or

145

tomorrow, but I don't think we have months."

"Noah—"

When her voice trailed off, he felt his frustration morph. He couldn't get the illusion system working. And he was afraid, deep down, that he couldn't get this woman to love him.

"I'm falling in love with you," he said baldly.

She jerked back a little, her wide eyes on his face.

"Well?" he demanded.

She looked away. "You kind of sprung it on me."

Her face was in profile, but he could see it. Fear written all over her.

"This is where the going gets tough, Laura." He spun her to face him. "This isn't just about fun, games, and fucking anymore."

Say something, he wanted to shout. Instead, she had that look on her face, the one she used to hide her true feelings.

"I had a woman who just wanted good times." He spat the words out. "I don't need another."

He saw the color drain out of her cheeks. He knew it was unfair, she hadn't made him any promises. Hell, she'd told him she didn't want to risk a relationship and he'd still pushed her.

But right now he felt like he was drowning, and he needed her. He needed more from her.

He was afraid it was more than she had to give.

"We both know you wanted parts of me...but not everything."

She'd obviously given Jake her everything. All she'd given Noah was her body.

And he wanted her heart.

Silence.

Noah's chest constricted. "This is where you say something."

She swallowed. "I'm not sure what you want me to say."

Those words arrowed under his skin. Damn, they hurt. "I want you to tell me how you feel. I don't need you to spout platitudes to make me feel better, I just want the truth."

Confusion crossed her features and he realized she really didn't have anything to say to him.

He felt the ground shift under him. He'd been falling in love with Laura Bladon, and she'd just been having fun, while keeping her heart locked up tight.

"If you won't give yourself to me, all of you, we're done."

All emotion slid out of her face, leaving a composed mask. "Just like that."

"You aren't a coward, Laura. I know you've suffered, but you must know we're good together."

"Noah—" Her voice was soft, sympathetic.

Fuck. This was his last chance to reach her, to offer her the full truth. "I lied before. I'm not falling in love with you, I'm already there. Completely. One hundred percent."

She flinched and looked like he'd hit her.

And there was his final answer.

He sucked in a deep breath. "And you don't feel the same way. Right. Fine. Look, I have work to do." He stepped back, his insides feeling like a shredded mess torn up by raptor claws. "If you finally find the courage to see what's right in front of your face, come find me. If I'm still around, or still alive."

He walked toward the entrance back to the base. At the door, he paused. "Every day is precious, Laura." He wanted to storm back to her, drag her into his arms, and make her admit that she felt something for him.

Instead, he didn't look back.

He walked away. He had an illusion system to work on. And if there was one thing in life that had never let him down, never made him feel unworthy no matter how challenging it got, it was his work.

Noah made it back to the Swift Wind facility and threw himself into his work. If his tech team noticed he was working like a man possessed, they didn't mention it. When it got dark and the others headed back to dinner and their families and their beds, Noah stayed. He worked all night and into the next day.

Laura never came to see him.

"You trying to make yourself sick?"

Elle's voice made Noah lift his head out from under the propped open cover of the illusion system. He bumped the back of his head on the metal cover and he swore.

"Danny told me you've been working for two days and nights straight."

"So?"

"Noah, you've yelled at me when I've become obsessed with my work."

"Don't have to now. Marcus just tosses you over his shoulder and carts you off."

Elle's lips twitched for a second. "Then maybe I should have a word with a certain captain. I'm sure she'll do the equivalent."

His heart felt like a lump of rock. He picked up his tools and looked back at the system. "I'm sure she wouldn't care."

"Oh?" Elle's voice was laden with a multitude of different emotions. Curiosity the loudest.

"We're done."

"No."

"She's too scared to risk loving again, Elle. I can't force her to feel something she doesn't."

"That woman looks at you with such...longing. She cares, Noah, I know she does."

"Not enough." Damn, it was like ripping the wound open afresh and letting it bleed all over the place. "Maybe we're just too different. The straitlaced captain who loved and lost, and the geek who thought he was in love, but was really just a big idiot."

"Opposites attract, Noah."

"Yeah, but I don't think they can stay together."

"Marcus and I proved that wrong. I love him so much."

Yeah, they were opposites who somehow clicked. But that didn't promise the same for others. "Can we talk about something else? Please?"

"Sure." She leaned closer. "What's going on here?"

"Heart of the system is burned out." He pointed

at the charred and blackened parts. It made his gut harden. So much damage. "I don't have all the parts I need to rebuild it. And even if I did, the alien cubes put off too much power. They'd just burn out again."

"So you need stronger materials? That can withstand the extra energy?"

"Yes, but also something that fits with the existing systems." He froze. "Hell."

"What?"

"Maybe...what if—" He hurried over to his desk and snatched up some alien parts. Bits from genesis tanks and some alien comp screens. "What if I add the alien tech into ours?" He lifted a bunch of standard wiring. "Opposites in almost every way, but if I can combine them the right way, they could be the right combination. And be stronger for it."

Elle tilted her head. "Like you and the captain."

He released a breath. "I want us to be together so badly I can't think straight."

"Let me guess, you issued one of your straight-talking ultimatums?"

He winced. "I wanted to know how she felt."

"So you pushed and prodded and demanded?" Elle asked. "On top of you suffering from a lack of sleep and a huge disappointment after the failed test."

Shit. "I was an asshole." Maybe Laura had deserved some of what he said, but if he really loved her, he should have given her some time. A chance to take it all in without him hammering at her, demanding, and throwing down his ultimatums. "Shit."

"You'll win her back, Noah."

"Yeah, but right now, I need this illusion system working to keep everyone safe." To keep Laura safe. And she needed some time and hell, maybe he did too.

"I'll leave you to it. Marcus will be looking for me."

"Thanks, Elle."

She smiled. "Any time. I'm used to dealing with hardheaded males who need a little sense talked into them occasionally." A cheeky grin. "I'm getting pretty darn good at it."

After she'd left, Noah set to work on splicing the alien tech into the guts of the illusion system. There was a risk it wouldn't work and he'd do more damage, but it was time to take a risk. He worked, took a few cat naps in his desk chair, and worked some more. But he ran into trouble after trouble, and preliminary tests showed it just wasn't working. Frustrated, he decided it was time to call on the one person who had successfully spliced alien tech into the base's systems. He reached for his comp and made a call.

"What?" Reed's grumpy voice answered.

"I need Natalya."

"She's taken," Reed growled. "Find your own woman."

"I need her brain, not her body."

"All of her is mine."

Noah heard a feminine voice in the background and figured Reed was getting a few choice words from his fiancée. "She did work splicing alien tech into the solar power system. I need her help."

"It's four am, Kim."

It was? He glanced at his watch. "Shit. Sorry. But I still need her help. It's for the convoy illusion system. I'm not just trying to use the energy cubes to power our system, I want to completely embed them into it."

Reed muttered something unintelligible, and a second later, Natalya came on the line. "I'll be there shortly." Her voice was sleepy, and he heard a light Russian accent that he didn't usually notice. "Just let me take a hot shower first because I need to wake up."

"Woman loves her showers," Reed said. "I'll walk her down to the convoy."

"Thanks, Reed."

Noah ended the call and sat back in his chair. He wondered what Laura was doing. Was she asleep? Did she miss him? Was she hurting as much as he was? He exhaled loudly. Shit, maybe that was why he didn't want to go back to his quarters. He didn't want to sleep without her. Smell her on his sheets.

He looked at the illusion system. Natalya would be here soon and hell, this idea had a real shot at working. Months of work could be done in days.

He'd get some work done, then he'd go find his captain.

Chapter Thirteen

She missed him.

Laura sat at her desk in her office, staring off into space. Katrina was working with her today, and the woman had asked Laura about a dozen times if she was okay.

She'd nodded every time, but no, she wasn't okay.

She missed Noah, and it was killing her to stay away from him.

But he wanted things from her. He wanted everything from her. She wasn't sure if she could give him her heart and soul.

She'd heard through the base grapevine that he'd had some breakthrough, and was having some success repairing the illusion system. That was good news. She was happy for him.

Laura looked down and realized she was doodling on her notepad. Actually, she'd been sketching. A picture of Noah stared back at her, with his brows drawn down in concentration, and his pirate eyes staring intently.

There was a loud grunt and shout from outside her door. She sighed. Katrina was with their newest prisoner. A large raptor found not too far from Blue Mountain Base. Laura was guessing he was a scout of some description. But so far, he was proving very resistant to questioning and was particularly aggressive.

There was a knock on Laura's door. "Come in."

Katrina popped her head in. "Our guest is not very happy."

"So I can hear. He give you any info?"

The woman pulled a face. "Not a thing."

"We'll keep working on him. How's Gaz'da?"

"Compared to the new raptor, he's a sweetheart."

"All right. Grab a coffee, then have another run at the new raptor."

"I'm calling him Scrooge."

Laura smiled for the first time since Noah had walked away from her. "Let me know if you need a hand."

"Roger that." Katrina cleared her throat. "Laura, are you sure you're okay? You seem...down."

Laura thought about opening up and talking about Noah. But she couldn't do it. "I'm working through a few things."

"You and Noah have a fight?"

Laura stiffened.

Katrina waved a hand. "You didn't think people knew that you and the sexy head of the tech team were doing the dirty? We deal in information around here, remember?"

Laura gave a slow nod.

"You hang on to that one. He's smart and sexy,

and looks at you like he wants to eat you all up. That wasn't easy to find before the aliens came, and now—" Katrina shrugged. "You're lucky."

After the woman had left, Laura sat there staring at the closed door. She was lucky. She'd loved once, and she'd lost. But now she was getting another chance.

She just had to find the courage to grab her happiness and not let it go.

She needed to talk to Noah. As soon as her shift was over, she was dragging him out of the Swift Wind facility and into bed. It was a good place to start.

The lights went off.

Her office was pitch black, and she couldn't see a thing. She suppressed the tiniest twinge of panic and counted silently in her head. *One. Two. Three.* The backup power kicked in, and the dim emergency lights positioned near the floor flickered on.

Katrina appeared again. "Laura?"

"Everything okay out there?"

"Backup power is on and all the cells are secure. What's happening? Another emergency drill? They springing surprise ones on us now?"

"I guess. Stay alert and watch the prisoners."

Katrina nodded and dissolved into the darkness.

Laura tapped her fingers on her desk. According to the memos she'd received with the drill schedule, no more evac simulations were planned for today. She cocked her head and listened. She was sure she could hear the distant peal of alarms.

She put a call through to the Ops Area. The general and his team would be up there.

There was no answer.

Damn. Her pulse raced. This wasn't good. She'd have to go and see what the hell was going on. She stood, and at that moment, the emergency lights failed.

Her heart clamored in her chest. Oh, God. That meant the backup power had failed.

And that also meant the electronic locks on the cells would have failed. Leaving only deadbolts securing the doors.

Laura grabbed her laser pistol and headed out to find Katrina.

It was so damn dark. Her laser pistol had a small light attached to the end of it, but she was worried about announcing her location. She opened her door slowly. The darkness was impenetrable. She moved, using her memories of the floor plan, and keeping one hand against the wall.

A hushed, pregnant silence filled the air.

"Katrina," she whispered.

No response.

Laura kept moving.

Then she stumbled over something on the floor.

She crouched, feeling around. She felt a body. Felt something sticky on her fingers. Felt long hair.

No. No. Risking showing her location, she flicked on the tactical flashlight attached to her pistol. It illuminated Katrina's blank face. She was lying on her side, a pool of blood beneath her. Her stomach was a mass of bloody scratches.

Caused by raptor claws.

Laura looked up. Saw the nearest cell door was open. The deadbolt ripped from the wall.

She flicked off her light and sat there, crouched in the dark.

She was alone in here with two enemy raptors and an alien bug.

She dragged in a steadying breath. Whatever was happening above, she couldn't let these aliens escape and get into the base.

Just then, the ground rumbled around her. She heard distant bangs. Explosions.

There was no mistaking it now.

The aliens were attacking Blue Mountain Base.

A grunt sounded in the darkness and Laura froze.

She turned her head. Just as an enormous body slammed into her.

They crashed into the ground, and she fought to get her laser pistol up.

The raptor let out a roar.

***

Noah sprinted through the tunnels.

They were filled with smoke, screams, and running, panicked people.

"Get to the exits," he yelled. He waved a group on, pointing to the exit he'd used to get in.

There'd been no raptors there.

But there were raptors everywhere else.

As he'd sprinted to the base from the Swift Wind

facility, he'd seen a fleet of pteros in the sky, dropping bombs.

Even now, the base was vibrating from the explosions above.

Raptor troops were in the base. They'd known where the main entrances were hidden and had blown the doors off.

Right now, all he could think of was getting to Laura.

He kept running, covering his mouth when the smoke got thick. He yelled at some more residents to get above—a man and a woman with two small, frightened children.

"Follow your evacuation plan. Get to the convoy."

They nodded and hurried away.

With Natalya's help, Noah had finished work on embedding the cubes into the illusion system...but he hadn't had time to test it yet.

He had no idea if it would work or not.

All he could do was pray, and hope Lady Luck decided to smile on him for a change.

She'd given him Laura. Sure, they'd screwed up, but he was going to find her and drag her out of here. After that, he wasn't letting her go.

He rounded a corner and saw the door to the comp lab ahead. It was open. And he heard grunts and guttural shouts from inside. As well as things smashing.

He hesitated. He had to go past it.

After drawing a deep breath, he ran.

But he looked, saw the huge raptors inside.

There was no smoke in the lab, so he had a perfect view of them stomping on all of his comps and tools and supplies with their thick, heavy boots. He saw one raptor swing a massive arm, and the shelf behind Noah's desk collapsed. His dice scattered across the floor.

And a second later, that raptor turned his head, his red gaze colliding with Noah's.

Noah kept running. He heard the raptors shouting and spilling into the tunnel behind him.

Fuck. He wasn't going to make it.

Green poison sprayed the tunnel walls beside him, hissing as it burned through the concrete.

He tensed, waiting to feel it burn through his skin.

Suddenly, black-clad bodies ran out of the smoke ahead. Green laser fire whizzed through the tunnel.

Squad Nine appeared. The women—with set faces and their weapons up and aimed—moved forward. Mac, Taylor, Cam, Sienna. They moved like one, pressing forward.

Roth and Theron appeared behind them, just as focused, their gazes on the raptors.

Noah risked a glance back. Saw the raptors ducking for cover.

"Noah!" Roth shouted. "Get the hell out of here. Get to an exit."

With a nod, Noah turned the corner. He could still hear the sounds of Squad Nine and the raptors fighting.

But he wasn't headed upward. He was headed down.

He took the spiral ramp down to the prison area. Here, the sounds of the fighting and the explosions were muffled. Noah moved slower now, creeping along the edge of the tunnel.

It was as black as the densest, moonless night down here. He sucked in a breath. This sector had lost backup power. Jesus. That meant the cells would be unsecured.

And far too easy for a huge, strong alien to bust down the doors.

He grabbed his small flashlight out of his pocket and flicked it on. The thin shaft of light illuminated the door to the prison. He crept toward it. The door was still closed.

Where was the guard? He glanced around but only saw dark shadows.

His boots hit something.

He glanced down and then recoiled. The guard's body. Chewed and clawed.

Fuck. He scrambled over to the wall. He knew there was a rack of the stun weapons the prison guards used here somewhere. He ran his hands over the wall.

He touched the rack, and yanked a stunner off. He turned.

Just as a giant, dog-like thing leapt at him from the darkness.

Noah fired the stunner. The canid growled. His flashlight illuminated rows of long teeth in a rabid mouth. Noah kept firing and the canid smashed into him. They skidded across the floor.

But Noah felt hot anger flowing in his blood. He had to get to Laura, and this thing was in his way. He jammed the stunner into the creature's mouth and pressed the trigger again.

The canid squealed, leapt off him, turned in an ungainly circle, then collapsed.

Noah jumped up and raced for the prison door.

He touched a hand to it. It was closed, but he saw that there were no lights blinking on the electronic lock.

Then he heard a chilling sound on the other side of the door.

The deep, guttural barks of alien laughter.

Chapter Fourteen

Laura strained against the raptor. It had her pinned. She'd lost her laser pistol somewhere, and the raptor had sunk its claws into her belly, shredding her clothes and skin.

There was no pain, but she was bleeding.

She felt the alien's hot breath in her face. She knew the thing was toying with her, and his laughter told her he was clearly enjoying himself.

She was going to die here, in the dark, alone.

Her thoughts turned to Noah, and she wanted to scream. They'd wasted time they could have spent together. She'd wasted time because she was afraid.

The thoughts fueled her anger. She thrust everything she had into fighting the raptor. Her pistol wasn't far away. She could see the thin beam of light from the tactical flashlight attached to it.

Get it. Kill the raptor. Escape.

She heaved against the creature's bulk. He wouldn't budge.

Suddenly, another body barreled into the fight. Her raptor attacker grunted and rolled off her.

Laura scrambled into a crouch, and snatched at her laser pistol. She spun and faced the person who'd helped her.

Her heart clenched. It was no person. It was Gaz'da.

Gaz'da had the large raptor pinned. They strained against each other, snarling.

"Captain," Gaz'da said in a strained voice.

She raced over and aimed the laser pistol. Her hands were shaking a little, but they were steady enough. Green laser lit up the darkness. She held the trigger down until the large raptor fell backward. He landed on the ground, his last breath making a wheezing sound before he went still.

Laura swayed on her feet. Pain crept in now, a savage burning through her middle. Her arm holding the pistol fell to her side. "Gaz'da, are you okay?"

The raptor nodded. "You are not."

He was right. She felt dizziness wash over her. Then she heard the bang of a door.

"Laura!" Noah sprinted in and skidded to a stop. He was holding a stunner prod in his hands. He took one look at her, then Gaz'da, then lifted the weapon.

"No." She held out a hand. "Gaz'da saved my life."

Noah's gaze went to the dead raptor on the floor.

Laura's legs gave out. Noah cursed and was there, helping her back against the wall. "Shit, honey. You're bleeding all over the place."

She heard concern in his voice and wished she could see him better. She could barely make out his features in the dim light. "You came for me."

He cupped her cheek. "Of course I did. I always will."

She nodded, but the pain was starting to steal her breath now.

"Where's the first aid kit?" he asked.

"My office."

"Hang on." He touched her lips.

There was movement and Gaz'da knelt beside them. Laura felt Noah stiffen, but he didn't move.

"Thank you, Gaz'da," she said quietly. "For saving me." She'd been his jailor, his interrogator, his enemy. And yet, he'd saved her life.

The alien nodded.

Noah looked torn, but he stood. "I'll be right back." He sent a pointed look at the raptor, then was swallowed by the shadows.

Gaz'da was frowning at the floor. It had always been hard to read his face, but now he looked upset. "I was...not always Gizzida."

She'd guessed as much. He obviously hadn't been human, but probably some other race captured and turned by the Gizzida.

"I'm sorry. For what they did to you. For what I've done to you."

"You were...fair. Especially considering the—" he paused, searching for the word "—circumstances."

Noah returned and started yanking things from the first aid kit. "The base has been attacked. We're evacuating."

What the hell was she going to do with a raptor prisoner who was victim, ally, and enemy all rolled into one? "Gaz'da—"

"I do not belong with humans," the raptor said. "And I have no desire to go back to the Gizzida."

"Then you're free, Gaz'da," Laura said. "Go. Find a way out and then go somewhere far away from here."

The alien tilted his head, then nodded.

Noah set to work stopping Laura's bleeding. As he applied pressure to her belly, she sucked in a sharp breath. The pain had her breaking out in a sweat.

"Sorry." He touched her cheek for a second. Then he looked at Gaz'da. "Head for one of the exits on the southern side of the base. The ones closest to the prison area. They weren't part of our evacuation plan. You need to be careful. Humans will be fighting the raptors. They'll shoot at you."

"Thank you." Gaz'da looked at Laura. "You were an evenhanded captor. I was never mistreated. Goodbye, Captain Bladon."

Her chest hitched. "Goodbye, Gaz'da."

The alien stepped into the darkness and was gone. Laura leaned back against the wall. Despite Noah trying to stop her bleeding, she felt the puddle of blood beneath her growing.

There was no way she'd make it out of the base.

But Noah's face was set in hard lines as he worked to stem the bleeding. She stared at the planes of that face she'd come to know so well. God, she was still so angry about the wasted days and harsh words between them. All because she'd been trying to protect herself.

And it was far too late. He was already under her skin, in her heart.

She could have been with Noah these last few days, instead of locked in her office, hurting anyway.

Now she felt the life bleeding out of her. She swallowed. Now she was really afraid. She wondered if Jake had been afraid at the end. She hoped not.

"Bleeding's mostly stopped." Noah's voice was grim. He dabbed some med gel on and was taping bandages over the wounds. "That'll have to do, because we need to get out of here."

As if to underscore his words, the base shook around them.

"I'm going to give you a painkiller." He pressed an injector to her neck. "We need to get out and get to the convoy."

She grabbed his hand. "Noah...we both know I'll never make it."

"Honey, we're in this together." He cupped her cheeks, forcing her to meet his gaze. "Whatever happens. No more running from each other, no more lies, no more ultimatums. It's you and me, whether you like it or not."

Even in these dire circumstances, she smiled. "Really?"

"Yep, whatever happens." He got an arm around her back. "Ready?"

"Ready."

He hauled her to her feet. She felt a sickening wave of dizziness but gritted her teeth. The pain was ebbing, the drugs easing it away.

She had to do this. Because she knew from the obstinate tone in Noah's voice that if she didn't go, he'd stay with her.

And then they'd both die.

She had to get him out.

She braced herself. "Let's go."

***

Noah kept his arm tight around Laura as they headed out of the prison area. She was limping badly, each one of her breaths a harsh inhalation.

A muscle ticked in his jaw. He was getting her out of here, one way or another.

It was slow going up the spiral ramp. As they neared the top, he heard screaming and the sounds of fighting.

And the sounds of the raptors.

He also smelled smoke. His gut cramped. The base—their home and haven—was being torn apart.

Noah gripped the laser pistol in his right hand harder. *Just get to the convoy.* That was the only thing he could focus on right now.

"Ready to move?" he asked.

She looked up at him. Pain had etched deep lines on her face. "No. But I will give it everything I've got."

He didn't doubt it. "Go."

They hobbled forward. Noah tried to take as much of her weight as he could. He led them down empty tunnels when he could, but finally, they reached one where he heard fighting around the corner, and they had no option but to go through.

He paused and peeked around.

His chest went hard. He saw base residents battling raptor soldiers. Lasers were firing and raptor poison was eating into the walls. Dead bodies—mostly human, he realized, his chest hurting—littered the ground.

Just get to the convoy.

"Come on." He held her tighter and they moved toward the melee. The smoke shrouded them, and the crazy fighting did, too.

Then one raptor spun and spotted them. He let out a vicious snarl.

Noah shot him in the face.

They hurried on. Noah caught a glimpse of Chef—the big man in charge of the base's cooking—wrestling an alien to the ground. God. For a single second, Noah slowed, caught between wanting to get Laura to safety...and wanting to help Chef.

Then Laura gasped.

Ahead, three large raptors rounded the corner at a run.

Shit. Noah fired. One raptor stumbled, but the others kept coming. He set Laura against the wall.

The first raptor charged him. Noah heard Marcus' voice in his head, talking him through his fight moves.

Noah slammed a kick into the raptor's side, and when the creature grunted and leaned forward, he followed through with a hard punch to the face.

Pain reverberated up Noah's arm, but he ignored it. He aimed the pistol toward the alien's chest and fired.

As the raptor fell, he saw the other one headed for Laura. She'd snatched up a raptor weapon from the ground and was holding it steady.

The raptor kept coming. Laura fired.

The green goo splattered across the alien's chest, and he let out an inhuman snarl as he dropped to the ground.

Noah ducked around him, grabbed Laura and yanked her down the tunnel.

As they moved, he felt her steps get slower, less coordinated.

"Come on, honey. We're making good progress."

"Liar." She drew a deep breath. "We aren't even halfway." Her face fell. "There will be more raptors between us and the exit."

"We'll make it."

"Noah—"

"We'll make it. Now shut up."

But soon Laura slowed to a walk. A quick glance down made his heart slam against his chest. Her shirt and trousers were soaked with blood.

They were nearing the end of a tunnel when he heard a strange clicking sound.

The sound echoed around them, raising the hairs on his head. They slowed and Noah glanced over his shoulder.

A creature stepped into view, its gaze on them. It walked on its back feet, with a long tail for balance. It was big, covered in feathers, and while the teeth in its mouth were large enough to cause nightmares, it was the huge, sickle-shaped claw on each hind foot that made Noah's blood run cold.

"Don't run," Laura whispered. "Velox."

The damn thing had "predator" stamped all over it, and right now, they were the prey.

Noah and Laura backed up slowly.

The velox stepped closer.

"They're fast, Noah. Hell Squad have tackled a couple. They aren't easy to take down."

And Noah had a laser pistol and Laura was injured. *Dammit to hell.*

He raised the gun. Whatever happened, he was fighting. For himself, for Laura, for a chance to live. It was time for Lady Luck to be fucking kind to him for a change.

The velox screeched and charged.

Noah shoved Laura hard. She fell, but she was out of the way.

He held his ground. "Come on, then, you feathered freak!" He fired the laser. It didn't even make the alien slow down.

He braced himself.

The sound of laser fire was a deafening roar in the tunnel.

The velox's body shuddered under the impact, then flopped forward onto the floor. Twitching.

Its feathered head landed an inch from Noah's boots.

He looked up...and saw Hell Squad moving forward, weapons raised.

Noah had never seen a more beautiful sight. "Damn glad to see you guys."

Marcus stepped ahead of his squad. "What the hell are you doing down here? You should be with the convoy." Then the soldier's gaze fell on Laura. She was sitting up but clutching her stomach, blood coating her hands. "Dammit. Shaw?"

The sniper hurried forward and knelt beside Laura. "Hey, sweetheart. Got yourself a little nick, there?"

Laura gave a hiccupping laugh. "Paper cut."

Shaw's lips twitched. He pulled out some sealers from his field first aid kit and shoved the shredded, sodden remains of Noah's handiwork aside. "Well, then, this sealer will suck onto your skin and stop that bleeding in a second."

"Thanks."

"Noah." Marcus' voice was low and urgent. "Raptors are pouring into the base." He cast a grim look at Laura.

"I'm not leaving her!"

Marcus made a frustrated sound. "Never said that. We'll help you get as far as we can."

Noah nodded. "Thanks."

"The old ventilation shaft will be safest. Not too many aliens at that end of the base."

Noah frowned. "It's a long ladder to the surface." It would be hell on Laura.

"Then you carry her if you have to."

Yeah, he would. With a nod, Noah helped Laura onto her feet. He heard her try to muffle her pained groan and he squeezed her arm. "We'll get to the convoy, and get Doc Emerson to look you over. You'll be fine."

Laura shot him a wan smile.

They moved through a few tunnels, dodging burning piles of debris and dead bodies, slowly making their way to safety. Noah stared at the bodies—both raptor and human as he passed. He recognized a few faces, but there was no time for grief right now.

He only prayed that most people had made it to the convoy. And that his untested illusion system would work.

They rounded a corner.

"Incoming," Cruz yelled.

Noah swiveled his head. A huge group of raptors was headed their way.

"Move faster," Marcus shouted.

Noah tried, and he knew Laura was using every last bit of willpower she had to stay on her feet.

"Noah!"

Her cry made him look forward.

More raptors were emerging from the smoke in the opposite direction.

They were trapped.

Chapter Fifteen

Laura smelled the harsh stench of smoke in her nostrils, heard Hell Squad and Noah firing their weapons, and felt the excruciating agony of her injuries. But all of her senses were muted, as though she were moving through a fog.

She saw the raptors moving in, firing their weapons. Marcus was roaring orders. She blinked and everything came back into focus.

"Laura? Laura? Stay with me." Noah's face pressed close to hers. "Hell Squad will keep the raptors busy, and we need to get past them."

She nodded. Even with the pain tearing through her, she loved looking at him. The pain was real, what she felt for him was real, and however long they had together, it was all worth it.

And she wanted more.

She was going to fight for more.

"Ready?"

She nodded, gathering the last of her reserves. *Get to the exit. Get to the convoy.* She chanted the mantra in her head. Then Noah would be safe.

Marcus and Cruz flanked the pair of them. Cruz snatched a grenade off his belt and activated it.

"On three," he said. "One, two, three!" He tossed the grenade.

Noah and Laura ran. Behind them, the grenade exploded with a loud bang, and Marcus and Cruz directed their fire at the oncoming raptors. Laura glanced back and saw the rest of Hell Squad fighting the aliens coming from the other direction. Shaw was taking the enemy out with steady headshots, Gabe was fighting hand-to-hand, Reed was lobbing a grenade, and Claudia was closest to the raptors, firing a carbine and a laser pistol at the same time.

"Go!" Marcus roared.

Noah pulled her forward. She focused on getting past the raptors.

A raptor lunged at them and fell under a hail of fire. They kept running, jumping dead bodies and other debris.

"Fuck you, asshole!" Claudia's voice.

"Let her go!" Shaw yelled.

Noah and Laura looked back. A raptor had a struggling Claudia clamped in his arms. She was thumping him on the head and fighting like crazy. Shaw was sprinting toward her, while the rest of Hell Squad were firing their weapons.

"Keep going, Noah," Marcus yelled.

"Come on." Noah tugged Laura onward.

They cleared the raptors, and ahead, she saw the small door into the ventilation shaft.

So close.

A pained cry came from behind them. Noah yanked the vent door open. "In."

Laura risked one last glance at Hell Squad.

She saw the raptor dragging Claudia backward now, his claws tangled in her hair. She was kicking and thrashing.

Hell Squad were converging.

Then a raptor tossed something.

"Grenade," Cruz yelled.

Hell Squad dove for cover. *Boom.* The tunnel filled with smoke and debris and the sound of falling rock. As it cleared, Laura saw the tunnel had partially collapsed.

Trapping Hell Squad on one side, and Claudia and the raptors on the other.

"No!" Shaw cried. He leapt up to the pile of rubble, tearing at it with his hands.

The others joined him, heaving at the tumbled chunks of rock and concrete.

"In, Laura," Noah said again. "We have to start climbing."

Her gut heavy as rock, she ducked into the narrow shaft. A long metal ladder speared upward. She set her boot on the first rung of the ladder, ignored her pain, and started climbing.

***

Noah reached past Laura and pushed the rusted hatch open.

The blinding afternoon sun made him blink. He pushed Laura ahead of him and out the top of the vent shaft, and then followed her.

175

Behind him, he heard Hell Squad coming up the ladder.

He cast a quick glance around the trees. Nothing was moving. No humans, no raptors. Only smoke pouring up from somewhere beyond the trees.

From memory, he calculated where the closest entrance to the convoy storage facility was.

Hell Squad climbed out of the shaft, one by one.

Claudia wasn't with them.

There was a grim and ugly silence. Every single one of them was aware Claudia was missing.

"Marcus, we need to go back," Shaw bit out. His jaw was locked so tight it looked like it might crack. "We have to find her."

"She was alive, Shaw. We'll get her back."

"They'll kill her!"

"She's valuable. They'll question her, first. Right now, our duty is to the base, to getting the residents out safely. There are kids, and sick people, old people, who need us more—" Marcus' voice cracked. "If you think it doesn't tear me up to leave her with those fuckers, even for a second..."

Shaw's hand clutching his rifle tightened until his knuckles bleached white. "They hurt her, and I'll track down every fucking alien responsible and gut them."

"Get in line," Gabe muttered. Something had nicked his head and blood covered half his face. He looked like something out of a horror movie.

"She's tough. She's smart," Marcus said. "She'll be fine, and we *will* get her out." He pinned a hard look at the sniper. "Got it?"

Shaw gave a jerky nod.

Marcus turned. "Gabe, can you carry Laura?"

"Sure thing." The big man moved over to Noah and Laura. "Okay with you, Laura?"

Laura looked like she was about to collapse. Noah was relieved when she nodded and Gabe swung her up in his arms.

They fell into a jog, Noah directing them through the trees. Soon, he found the disguised back entrance to the facility.

After the door slid open, uncovering a wide, descending staircase, he waved everyone inside. He cast a glance back toward the trees and, overhead, he saw even more smoke rising. He wanted to punch the wall in frustration, but instead, he passed through the door and made sure it was shut tight behind them.

Their boots echoed on the steps as they jogged downward. Soon, he heard the hubbub of voices, children sobbing, someone yelling.

Noah stepped into the Swift Wind facility and paused. His chest tightened. People milled around—they had black-stained faces, tangled hair, ripped clothes. Some had injuries. Some just stood or sat looking shell-shocked.

The convoy vehicles sat parked in a row, most with doors open and people moving in and out of them. Some people were in their assigned vehicles, while squad members in their armor were directing people to load up and get ready to leave. Near the medical vehicles, Noah spotted Emerson's blonde head and her team as they worked frantically to help the injured.

General Holmes strode toward them. His face was set like stone. "Hell Squad, Noah, Laura, I am so glad to see you."

"General," Marcus said.

His gaze tracked over them, then he frowned. "Where's Claudia?"

Marcus shook his head. "Raptors took her. But she's alive. As soon as the convoy is out of here safely, the squad and I are going back to get her."

The general looked like he wanted to argue, but finally he nodded.

"How is everyone?" Cruz asked.

"About as good as they look." The general's uniform was rumpled, black smoke stains smudged his chest, and there was blood on his hands. "But they're alive, and as long as we're alive and we have options, then we have hope." Something swam in the general's eyes. "We have lost a lot of people, though."

"What's the plan?" Noah asked.

"We need to get everyone loaded up. The raptors will figure we've gone somewhere, and soon they'll start searching. At least they dislike being in the trees." The general's blue gaze bored into Noah. "I know you haven't tested the illusion system, but what are the odds it'll work?"

Noah swallowed, his throat feeling like he'd swallowed barbed wire. "It's fifty-fifty."

The general sighed. "All right, then we'll risk staying put a little longer and leave at night. At least then we'll have the cover of darkness."

But they all knew the dark wouldn't be enough. It wouldn't scare the raptors away.

"Laura needs to see the medical team," Noah said.

"Go," the general said.

Gabe nodded and headed in the direction of the medical truck. Noah followed.

"Noah, we need to move soon," the general added. "I need you on the illusion system."

All he wanted was to be by Laura's side, but he nodded. "I'll be there."

He hurried over to where Gabe set Laura down. She sat on the concrete floor, her back against the medical truck. There just weren't enough stretchers and beds for all the injured.

A second later the doc appeared and crouched next to Laura. She looked harried, but focused. She took one look at Laura's stomach and hissed. "That has to hurt."

Laura managed a nod.

Noah slid down beside her and grabbed her hand. "She's lost a lot of blood."

The doc gave a firm nod. "Norah?" she called out. "Can you bring a shot of nanomeds? And we'll need some blood as well, please." Emerson cleaned the blood off Laura's stomach. "My nurse will give you the shots and bandage you up." The doctor pressed a hand over their joined ones. "I'm really happy you guys made it out."

"Noah...came back for me."

Laura's voice was husky. He tugged her into his side.

Emerson smiled. "I never doubted it."

After Norah, a round-faced woman with kind brown eyes and dark skin, had given Laura nanomeds and blood, she dressed the wounds. She handed a mini-tablet to Noah. "We're understaffed right now, so you'll need to monitor her nanomeds."

"Do we need to stay here?"

"No. But if there are any problems, call us. And take this." The nurse slapped an injector into Noah's hand.

"What is it?"

"The stim you'll need if the nanos go into cascade." The woman smiled and patted Laura on the shoulder. "Shouldn't need it, though. Nanos rarely go crazy and kill people anymore."

"Oh, good," Laura said.

Noah helped her to her feet, then he slid an arm behind her back. Before she realized his intent, he picked her up.

"Noah, you don't have exoskeleton armor that makes me easy to lift!"

He headed toward the tech truck. "I can manage."

He called out to many of his team. He was pleased to see most of them there, although a few were missing. He hoped grimly that they were simply with their families. A couple of techs were manning the comps inside the truck.

"Noah." Marin Mitchell shot to her feet. She was a tiny, curvy thing with a cute face and blonde curly hair. She didn't look like the expert comp hacker that she was.

"Hey, Marin. I need to get Laura lying down. You okay out here?"

The woman nodded. "No probs. I've worked with some of the drone operators, and we have a few drones peeping on the raptors."

"Nice work. I'll check in soon." Noah opened the door to his quarters and then closed it behind them, muffling all the external sound.

He set her down on the bed, flicked on a lamp built into the wall, and then urged her to sit.

Relief spread over her face instantly. "I should be helping."

"With what?" He pulled her boots off and nudged her to lie down.

"The prison bus. Check on my people. Something."

Noah checked the tablet, saw her nanomeds were working perfectly. He let out a breath. She'd be fixed up soon. "I'll check in on them for you. For now, all you need to do is rest and get your strength back."

"Noah...thanks for coming for me."

He leaned over her and cupped her face. Emotion was a tangled knot inside him. "I was an idiot for making demands of you before."

"No, you weren't. You were right. I was petrified and protecting myself." Her hand pressed over his. "Jake would have been disappointed in me. He would have been the first person to want me to live and find love again." She swallowed. "I love you, Noah."

Warmth spread through his chest. "I love you,

too, Laura. No matter what we face. No matter how this ends up, I want to spend however many minutes, hours, days we have together."

Her eyes glistened. "I'm all yours."

He stroked a hand down her arm. "Once you're better, we'll celebrate in style."

She raised a brow. "Champagne and a candlelit dinner?"

"I was thinking naked, and christening this new bunk of mine."

She laughed, but her eyelids drooped. "You're on, Kim. Shame you lost your dice collection. We could have played our game."

"Well..." He pulled open a drawer built in under the bed. He held up his hand and the lamplight glittered off a handful of dice.

"You stashed some in here?"

"Yep." He stroked a hand over her hair. "Let's get you out of those bloody clothes. You can shower later after you rest."

He helped her into one of his T-shirts and some sweatpants he had to cinch in tight at the waist on her. He'd just wadded up her bloody clothes and shoved them in the trash when the door slammed open. Noah looked over his shoulder. Marcus stood in the doorway.

"Raptors. Heading this way."

Noah shot to his feet. "What?"

"They must have tracked some survivors as they evacuated. They have some huge saws, and they're chopping down the trees to make pathways for their troops to move through. General's ordered us to leave. Now."

***

Laura sat up and then pushed to her feet. She was a little wobbly, but surprisingly, she felt much better already.

Noah scowled at her. "Back in that bed. Now."

She shot Marcus a look. "He's starting to sound a lot like you." She looked back at the man she'd fallen in love with. "No. I'm feeling better. You need to be in that illusion vehicle and I'm coming with you."

He swore and she ignored him.

"Is Hell Squad providing cover for the illusion system?" she asked.

Marcus nodded. "We'll be in one of the Hunters. Squad Nine will be in another."

"Excellent." She linked her arm through Noah's. "Come on. No time to argue."

He looked like he wanted to argue with her, but he went with her as they hurried to the illusion system vehicle. She saw the last of the residents climbing into vehicles. Some were still crying or looking confused, but others who were tasked with certain jobs were focused on firing up engines and manning weapons.

As the convoy's engines all started, the noise in the small space was deafening.

Noah yanked open the door on the illusion system truck. Laura climbed in the back seat and Noah got in with her. From here, they had access to the entire illusion system in the very back of the vehicle. She studied it and her eyes widened.

With all the alien tech spliced into it, the system now glowed with alternating red and orange colors. She couldn't begin to understand what he'd done, but it was amazing. The man was amazing.

"Austin, ready to go?" Noah called out.

Laura swiveled and saw a young man sitting in the driver's seat. She hadn't even noticed him. "Hi."

"Howdy," Austin said. "Everyone buckle up." He was maybe in his twenties, if he was lucky. He grinned. "I like to drive fast."

"He's the best driver on the tech team, so he volunteered to be driver for this vehicle," Noah said.

"And I haven't driven for a really long time." Austin patted the steering wheel. "Can't wait to get this baby going."

A blare of noise, like a fog horn, came over the vehicle's comm system. It cut off and then the general's voice followed.

"Today is a hard day for all of us. Again, we've lost friends, loved ones, our home. But we've prevailed before. We have survived everything the aliens have thrown at us, and we will prevail again today."

Laura reached for Noah's hand. His fingers clamped on hers, squeezed.

General Holmes continued. "We have a plan and now we will execute it. We can all get through this if we work together, and look out for each other. That is what the Gizzida keep underestimating.

Humanity's will to survive, to be free, and the innate strengths that make us human. We care, and we love, and we will fight to protect that." A pause. "Time to move out."

The lead vehicle started rumbling up the ramp. Laura knew the ramp led into a tunnel that would lead them away from the base. Not far, but hopefully it was far enough to escape the notice of the raptors.

Then it was their turn. Austin gunned the engine and they pulled forward. Noah squeezed Laura's hand one more time, then opened the window to the back of the truck. He climbed through.

"What are you doing?" she asked.

"I want to check everything again. Before I fire it up."

She nodded. He was so tense, the lines etched into his face appearing deeper, more permanent. She watched his long, clever fingers move over the illusion system.

He sat back and hunched his shoulders. "Well, we're as ready as we'll ever be."

"Tunnel exit coming up," Austin called back.

Laura's and Noah's gazes locked. This was another part of what being together meant. Not just the good times and the sexy times, it was being there for each other in the hard times as well.

The vehicle drove out into the dying day's light. Ahead, the lead vehicles were idling, waiting.

"Noah?" The general's voice on the comm. "Ready?"

"No," Noah muttered. He flicked some switches, dragged in a deep breath. "Here we go."

Laura heard a hum from the machine. She felt energy fill the air, the hairs on her arms rising. She looked out the windshield, staring at the trucks ahead.

"Everything still visible," the general said, his voice harsh. "No illusion."

"Dammit." Noah pressed his hands to his knees. "It's not working."

"Noah—" Laura tried to think of something to comfort him. Then the illusion system's hum changed, became a little more high-pitched.

"Goddamn thing will probably blow up now," Noah said.

"Get back in here." She waved to the seat beside her. She didn't want him sitting on the damn thing if it caught fire.

He climbed back in beside her.

"The rest of the convoy is coming out through the tunnel now," Austin said.

"You tried your best, Noah," she said quietly. "You couldn't have done anything more."

The whine of the illusion system increased to another, higher, pitch.

Excited voices came through the comm. A black vehicle roared up beside them, and through the windshield, she saw Hell Squad's armored Hunter.

"Kim, you are a genius," Marcus said on the comm. "We couldn't see you at all as we drove up. The illusion's working!"

Laura's breath caught in her lungs.

Noah leaned forward between the front seats and tapped the comm screen. "General?"

"It's working, Noah. You did it! Everyone, we're moving out. Stick together and stay in the illusion field."

Noah punched the back of the empty passenger seat, grinning. The general's command vehicle pulled out first, and the rest of the convoy fell into place. Austin maneuvered them into the center of the convoy, and they were flanked by two Hunters.

Laura nudged Noah. "Nice work."

He leaned back in the seat. "I knew it would work."

The arrogance forced a laugh from her. She decided not to mention his tense muscles and earlier frustration.

"How are you feeling?" he asked, concern darkening his eyes.

She'd been injured, the base had been destroyed, and they were on the run. She should be a wreck.

Instead... "I'm feeling pretty darn lucky."

He grinned at her. "Me, too, honey. Me, too. I'm a genius, I have one hell of a beautiful woman, and we're alive. Not too bad."

She couldn't resist the grin on his face, and she kissed him. He wrapped his arms around her and she sank into him.

Yes, despite all the bad, she was feeling like one lucky lady.

Chapter Sixteen

Shaw

Shaw Baird's hands clenched on the controls of the autocannon. Cruz was driving the Hunter and they were flanking the illusion system vehicle. There was a tense, charged silence in the Hunter.

The convoy had escaped the aliens. Shaw figured he should be jubilant. Instead, inside he was a fucking chaotic mess.

They'd left Claudia behind.

He wanted to yell, shout and pound on something. Preferably a fucking alien raptor.

Instead, he manned the cannon, and counted each kilometer they put between them and the smoking remains of the base…and Claudia.

It reminded him of another time he'd abandoned someone who mattered. Someone who hadn't survived long enough for him to return to get her.

His jaw clenched and he worked hard to draw in a calming breath through his tight chest and find a little bit of control. Claudia wasn't his sister. She was a tough, badass, superbly-trained fighter.

But she was his family.

Shaw's childhood had been...well, shitty didn't even begin to describe it. As soon as he could, he'd escaped and joined the Coalition military. Then he'd made his own family—first with the Special Air Service and now, with Hell Squad.

Hell Squad had given him everything he'd never realized he'd needed. They meant the damn world to him. And Claudia...

The mass of rage and pain in him made his fingers flex on the cannon controls. He wanted to shoot something. He itched to unload laser rounds into the enemy. He almost wished the raptors would find them.

The fucking bastards had her. If they hurt her... The thought of Claudia Frost dead—all that tough, vital life gone—made his jaw clench so hard his teeth hurt.

He'd never told her, but Claudia was his touchstone, that one thing in the world that made sense. She infuriated him, pulled him into line when he was an ass, she had his back in a fight and she made him laugh.

And now she was gone.

A slap on his boot made him look down from the elevated cannon seat.

Marcus' scarred face looked up. "Convoy's free of raptor pursuit. Elle says the aliens aren't headed this way."

Shaw's heart jumped. "We going to get her now?"

Marcus gave a sharp nod. "Hell yeah."

"About fucking time."

Marcus' gaze was intense. "We'll get her back."

As his leader disappeared from view, the Hunter executed a tight U-turn. Shaw got a quick glimpse of the assorted mix of vehicles in the convoy—trucks, SUVs, cars, converted buses. Ordinarily, he'd feel a twinge of guilt for leaving them. They were innocent civilians, survivors—men, women and kids who needed his protection.

He'd joined the military to escape his crappy home, but also for the chance to protect those who were weaker. Hell, he'd been protecting people all his life—keeping bullies off smaller kids in the school playground, taking his father's drunken slaps to protect his sister, rescuing pretty girls from the advances of assholes.

But today, he didn't have it in him to feel more than a fleeting blip of guilt.

Claudia needed him. And while she wasn't a civilian, and she sure as hell wasn't weak, and she liked to tell everyone she didn't need anyone's protection, she was damn well getting it today.

He stared at the fading white line in the center of the road as it whizzed beneath the Hunter.

I'm coming, Frost. You fucking hold on. I'm coming for you.

***

Noah gripped the steering wheel with one hand, and stroked Laura's hair with the other. She was slumped in the passenger chair beside him, fast asleep. Austin was in the back seat, stretched out, snoring softly.

They'd driven most of the night, and were now deep in the mountain forests, well south of Blue Mountain Base. It had been a long, slow, twisting route. There'd been a few tense moments as they'd escaped—pteros buzzing overhead, a detour to avoid raptor vehicles, and one convoy vehicle had broken down.

The people inside had been put into other vehicles and they'd abandoned the vehicle in a mountain ghost town. Hopefully, if the raptors found it, they'd think it had been in the town all along. The little town had been so pretty, and perfect...and empty.

Just ahead, he saw a Z6-Hunter cruising in front of them. Squad Nine. The other Hunter was long gone.

Hell Squad had stayed with the convoy for a couple of hours before turning back.

They were going to bring Claudia home.

Noah's hands flexed on the wheel. The raptors had to know Claudia was a member of Hell Squad. They wouldn't kill her straightaway. At least, he hoped not. Besides that, the woman was the definition of tough.

She'd make it. Strong women seemed to dig in and fight until they got what they wanted. No matter the odds. No matter the obstacles.

He glanced down at his own woman. Yep, he'd discovered he had a thing for tough women.

The comm crackled to life. "Swift Wind convoy, this is General Holmes." The general's voice was hoarse and he sounded exhausted. "We've identified a camping ground deep in the nearby national park. We'll be pulling in to take a break."

Laura stirred. "Where are we?"

"Headed into a national park campground."

She wrinkled her nose. "I hate camping."

Noah followed the convoy and soon, the vehicles were all pulling in and parking. Noah got out and stretched his stiff body. The general's team had done well. The place was covered in trees, which provided good cover. But he still checked the illusion system and made sure it was operational. Not far away, a river glimmered under the moonlight.

"We need to find the doc and get her to check your nanomeds and injuries," Noah said.

Laura nodded but was eyeing the vehicles and the people wandering around. "We've lost so many."

Yeah, it was easy to see they were several hundred people short. Anger was a hot arrow through him. The Gizzida would pay. For everything.

They might have won this battle, but the war wasn't over. If the aliens thought this would demoralize them, they were so very wrong.

General Holmes appeared. He'd lost his uniform jacket and looked tired, rumpled and stressed. "Drones are up. Finn and the quadcopters will be landing here shortly. How's the illusion system?

"Fully operational."

Holmes rubbed the back of his neck. "Great. I'll let everyone know they can light small fires."

"What's the plan from here?" Noah asked.

"We head to the Enclave."

The Enclave was the secret underground bunker built by the former Coalition President. Roth and Avery had been there and brought back data on it. From what Noah had seen of the schematics, it was well outfitted and secure.

It was also hundreds of kilometers away, south of Sydney. "It's a long way to go with a convoy like this," Noah said.

The general nodded. "But we can make it. My team has mapped out the best route, along with back-up plans, too. We'll take each day as it comes, and move safely and cautiously toward the Enclave."

Just having a plan and knowing where they were going made something in Noah settle. They could do this. He looked at the people around him. Spotted some kids chasing each other, playing tag and laughing. He saw an elderly couple sitting together on camp chairs someone had found for them. They were holding hands. He saw a young couple kissing, completely lost in each other.

Already, human resilience was shining through.

They'd survive.

"Well done on the illusion system, Noah." Holmes clapped him on the shoulder. "Now get some rest. I think I'll grab a nap too." He strode back toward the command truck.

Another small group of people appeared in the darkness. Roth Masters, his partner, Avery, and the rest of Squad Nine. With them were Santha, with an arm around young Bryony, Devlin, and Natalya.

"Any word from Hell Squad?" Noah asked.

Santha nodded. "Elle's in the comms truck. She's in contact with them." Santha's face was grim. "The aliens have picked over the base and moved on. They don't seem to know where we've disappeared to and have headed away from our direction. Hell Squad has found a few survivors."

"Claudia?"

Santha shook her head. "But they confirmed she's alive, and the aliens have taken her. Hell Squad is on the trail."

"And Hell Squad doesn't stop until they achieve their objective," Dev said.

"Hell yeah," Roth murmured.

"We are going to light a fire and cook some breakfast," Natalya said quietly. "You're welcome to join us."

Laura yawned. "I need to wash up, first."

"And then get some rest," Noah added. Right now, in the wake of all this, he wanted Laura to himself. "Rain check?"

"Sure." Natalya smiled, looking like she wasn't fooled one bit.

Noah winked at the woman, then turned Laura toward the tech truck. "Unfortunately, there isn't enough room for both of us in my shower unit. You go shower and find some fresh clothes." He smiled. "I stashed a few of your things in my quarters."

"Did you?"

"I'm going to send the doc over to check on you

and then I'm going to take a quick dip in the river." People were already down there, splashing. "Then we can celebrate this whole being in love thing."

"Sounds good," Laura said. "Very good." She disappeared into the truck.

Noah kept it quick. Emerson agreed to check in on Laura, and then after a dunk in the frigid water of the river, he ran around and begged, borrowed and stole the few things he needed.

Maybe he was crazy to be doing this in the aftermath of the base attack, but he wanted to show Laura that living and loving were important. No matter what.

He set everything up in his tiny quarters, listening to the shower running. For a second, memories assailed him. Laura bleeding all over the floor, both of them running through the base to escape, him praying the illusion system would work. He sank onto the bunk, surprised to find his hands a bit shaky.

More than anything, he needed Laura right now. He needed a reminder that they were both still alive.

She came out of the shower unit wearing another one of his T-shirts. She halted at the sight of him.

He sat back on the bed. "I told you some of your clothes were in the cupboard."

"I saw them, along with the sketchbooks, pencils and paints." She smiled. "Thank you."

"You're welcome."

She plucked at the gray T-shirt. "This seemed

far more comfortable...and comforting. Like your arms are wrapped around me."

"Come here." He tugged her down on the bed. "I'd prefer to really have my arms around you."

She snuggled into him.

"What did Doc Emerson say?" he asked.

"I'm in perfect health."

A tension he hadn't known he was carrying, eased. "Good."

Her gaze fell on the small table he'd set up. "Candlelit dinner?"

"Well, candlelit breakfast." A candle flickered in the center of the tiny table. And there were two plates with some eggs and protein substitute on them. "Couldn't find any champagne, though. Sorry."

Her hands pressed into his chest, her lips brushing his jaw. "Don't need it. I'm drunk enough on loving you."

With a growl, Noah pulled her head back and caught her mouth with his.

The desire flared into hot flames. An urgent need pumped through Noah. The need to claim her, feel her tight body around his cock, feel her heart racing because of his touch.

She felt it. "Noah."

"Now." He rolled her under him. "Hard. Fast."

"Yes." Her hands tangled in his hair.

Noah didn't waste time with any foreplay. He didn't have it in him right now. That urgent need turned to a pounding roar in his head. He tore his trousers open. When he pushed up the T-shirt she wore, he found her gloriously bare.

He made a sound—part groan, part growl. He shoved her thighs apart and moved over her. When she tried to wrap her legs around him, he caught one of her knees and yanked it high. He sank deeper into the cradle of her hips, and she moaned.

Then he thrust inside her.

She cried out. "Noah!"

Yes. This was what he needed. He pounded into her. "You and me, Laura. Always."

"Always." She gasped the word.

He had to go faster, harder. Noah flexed his hips. He increased his pace, tension growing in his body. He kept his gaze on hers. He wanted her to feel everything, wanted her to savor each brilliant sensation.

Her fingernails dug into his scalp and she arched beneath him. She dragged her hands over his shoulders, and he felt those nails rake his back. As her release shattered her, she let out a hoarse cry.

Noah plunged into her again, one more time, then he held himself there, snug inside her. He throbbed, felt the hot pulses as he came. He groaned her name.

They stayed there, destroyed, wrapped in each other for a long time. Here, there were no aliens, only the gentle pleasure of listening to the quiet breaths of the person you loved, and feeling the beat of their heart against yours.

"I love you, Laura." He pressed his lips to her hair. "I am really, really glad Lady Luck decided to

ANNA HACKETT

stop being a bitch."

"Me too." Laura pressed a kiss to his chest. "I'm so glad I'm alive. And living again."

Noah vowed he'd dedicate himself to making her feel as much pleasure as he could. Every day. "Yes, I'm feeling *very* lucky. Not only did I hide an entire convoy from alien invaders—" he tightened his hold on her "—I tamed the dragon."

Her fingernails dug into him again. "You call me that name again and I'll—"

"You'll what?"

She shoved him, rolling him beneath her. God, she was beautiful. Her legs clamped down on either side of his hips.

"Why don't I show you?" she whispered silkily.

"Do your worst, Captain Dragon." Because Noah knew wherever they were, whatever happened, he'd love every second of it.

I hope you enjoyed Noah and Laura's story!

Hell Squad continues with SHAW, the story of smart-mouthed sniper, Shaw Baird and the woman he's desperate to save.

Don't miss out! For updates about new releases, action romance info, free books, and other fun stuff, sign up for my VIP mailing list and get your *free box set* containing three action-packed romances.

Visit here to get started:
www.annahackettbooks.com

FREE BOX SET DOWNLOAD

JOIN THE ACTION-PACKED ADVENTURE!

Formats: Kindle, ePub, PDF

Preview – Hell Squad: Shaw

The building was empty.

There was nothing here.

Shaw Baird slammed his combat boot into a rotted cardboard box and sent it skidding across the concrete floor. He and his squad were searching an abandoned factory. Before the alien invasion, it looked like it had made cars. Old conveyors and pieces of once-high-tech equipment filled the large space. But after a year and a half of being abandoned—as what was left of humanity ran to avoid the raptor aliens—the machines were now sagging and rusty.

And up until a few hours ago, the raptors had been using the place to hold human prisoners.

Shaw's fingers tightened on his laser rifle. Something had tipped the scaly bastards off and they'd run.

Taking one of Shaw's squad mates with them.

Frustration boiled through him and he gave another box a kick. This one was filled with small metal parts. They clattered across the floor, making a huge din.

An ugly blackness welled in his gut. Over a week

ago, the aliens had invaded Blue Mountain Base—the haven the human survivors had made deep in an old underground military installation. Many had died, the place they'd called their home had been destroyed, and now they were all on the run. But during the attack, Claudia Frost—Hell Squad soldier and all-round badass—had been taken.

A large hand clamped down on Shaw's shoulder.

"We'll find her," a deep, gravelly voice said.

Shaw looked over at his squad leader. "It's been a fucking week, Marcus."

In that week, Shaw had barely slept, barely eaten. How could he rest when he knew Claudia was suffering? He'd seen the results of the aliens' testing and experimenting on human prisoners, and they weren't pretty.

"You need to keep it together," Marcus said quietly. "We won't stop until we find her, and I need you in top form to help us do that. *She* needs you."

That ugliness in Shaw ebbed and flowed, leaving a bitter taste in his mouth. He nodded. He'd already made a promise to himself, to her, that he would get her home.

"Over here," a voice with a touch of a Mexican accent called out.

It was Cruz, their second in command. Marcus and Shaw shared a brief glance, before they jogged over to where Cruz was crouched by the far wall.

"Fuck." Shaw's jaw tightened.

Hanging from a piece of equipment were two sets of makeshift chains. Shaw studied them. One set was smeared with blood and there were drops of blood on the floor.

He crouched, touching the sticky stain. It was still bright red. "Hasn't been here too long." He closed his eyes.

Cruz held a small hand-held scanner. It beeped. He looked up and nodded.

"She was here," Marcus said.

Shaw opened his eyes and saw his squad mates form up around him. Reed, the former Coalition Navy SEAL, and big, silent and deadly Gabe. Marcus and Cruz. They were all tough, tenacious soldiers and Shaw respected the hell out of them.

"We never leave anyone behind." Marcus' green gaze moved over all of them, before settling on Shaw. "We will *never* stop until we get her back." A muscle ticked in his jaw. "But for now, we have to head back to the convoy."

Shaw swallowed a curse. The human survivors from Blue Mountain Base had escaped the base attack in a motley band of outfitted vehicles. They were moving slowly through the mountains, hiding where they could. Thankfully, their head tech geek and electronics genius, Noah Kim, had gotten a huge-ass illusion system operational for the convoy. It essentially kept the convoy near-invisible from the aliens hunting them.

But the squads were still vital for protection and defense. Each team was cobbled together from any remaining soldiers who'd survived the invasion— Army, Navy, Air Force, Marines, Police. Hell, some fighters on the squads weren't even military. Squad

Three, known to everyone as the berserkers, were simply hardcore. They rushed in and fought with a crazy, wild abandon. Most of them were former bikers, mercenaries or possibly even criminals...sometimes it was best not to ask.

It didn't matter who you were before. Now everyone had to join together and find a way to help in the fight against the Gizzida.

He touched Claudia's blood again. What the hell were they doing to her? He exhaled a long breath. She was tough as nails. She'd been former Special Air Service like him. Funnily enough, they'd barely known each other before. She'd been on a different SAS team.

But now...now she was a vital piece of him. And he was only just realizing how vital since she'd been taken from him.

"So, who was in the second set of chains?" Reed asked, with his American twang.

"Don't know. But if they're still alive when we find Claudia, we take them too," Marcus said. Then he cocked his head, touching his ear. "Go ahead, Elle."

Elle Milton was their comms officer. The pretty brunette was sitting in a large truck with the convoy. The comms truck had been retrofitted with all the necessary equipment to let the squads' comms officers continue to do their jobs—feeding the squads intel, route information, and raptor numbers.

"Marcus, there is a lot of movement just south of your location," Elle said.

Shaw straightened. That had to be the raptors they were after.

"But that wasn't what I wanted to tell you." Her exhalation came across the line. "General Holmes needs you back here. There are raptor search patrols getting close to the convoy's current location. We need to move again, and we need Hell Squad back here."

Shaw bit his tongue. The protective part of him—the part born and honed by taking care of his little sister in the hellhole of their childhood—knew they had to protect the convoy. There were innocent kids and elderly people, mothers and fathers, scientists and doctors. People who had already been through so much. They needed the squads to keep them safe, especially now that they were on the run.

But a larger part of him wanted to go after Claudia.

She'd been in alien hands for a week. They all knew she was running on borrowed time.

The scar on Marcus' rugged face flashed white. "Back to the Hawk."

They formed up, but Shaw had to force his legs to move. Cruz took the lead, and they headed out.

Shaw kept a tight grip on his long-range laser rifle. *I'm coming, Claudia. Just hang on.* The rifle was a familiar touchstone under his hands, and helped him keep some control. He'd been surprised when he'd first joined the Army to discover he had a knack for sniping. He could read all the environmental factors, judge a shot, and stay steady through it all until the perfect time to finally pull the trigger.

Right now, he desperately wished for a raptor patrol to appear so he could take them down.

But as they jogged across cracked pavement, where straggly grass poked through the cracks here and there, and a sagging chain-link fence ringed the area that he guessed was once the employee parking lot, no raptors jumped out to attack. None of the various types of predator aliens the raptors used like attack animals came at them.

Ahead, the air shimmered. The Hawk quadcopter dropped its illusion, its dull, grey metal body shining in the morning sun. It ran on a tiny thermonuclear engine, with four rotors that were shrouded to reduce noise.

They climbed aboard and the pilot, Finn Eriksson, leaned back from the cockpit, scanning them. His mouth pressed together. "No luck?"

Shaw gave one savage shake of his head. "Missed her."

"Fuck." Finn sank back into his seat. "Strap in. Time to go home."

The Hawk's rotors turned and the quadcopter took off. Shaw knew Finn would have engaged the illusion system. While it didn't make them completely invisible, it blurred them to anyone who might be looking in their direction, messed with the Hawk's signature on raptor scans, and used directed sound waves to distort any noise.

It wasn't a long flight. They swept easily and quickly over the endless trees of the Blue

Mountains. He knew that behind them, to the east, lay the ruins of Sydney, once the capital of the United Coalition of Countries. Nations like the United States, India, and Australia had banded together to form the Coalition, and Sydney had been the jewel—a melting pot of people and cultures, a center for business, art, and pleasure.

And then the alien invasion had reduced it to burnt-out houses, shattered skyscrapers, broken landmarks.

Here in the mountains, staring down at the sea of trees, it was hard to imagine an alien apocalypse had occurred. But as they passed over small towns, it was easy to see there was no life. The towns were abandoned and still, ghosts of their former selves. Their former inhabitants were either dead, or captured by the aliens, or they'd fled, searching for shelter at places like Blue Mountain Base.

Or the Swift Wind Convoy, as they were now known.

The Hawk slowed and started its descent. Looking out, Shaw saw nothing but another abandoned ghost town, with an overgrown town square, and empty buildings with abandoned cars parked at skewed angles in the street.

But once they passed through the convoy illusion system and touched down, he saw what was being hidden.

Vehicles were parked in military precision outside what Shaw guessed had once been a school. Trucks, buses, and cars were all parked in a way that would let the drivers jump in and take off with a second's notice...a precaution, in case the aliens tracked them down and they had to evacuate.

Marcus pulled the side door of the Hawk open. "Get some rest. As soon as we get new intel, we're heading back out."

Shaw leaped out of the Hawk and instantly started pulling at his chest armor. Around him, he saw the survivors of Blue Mountain Base bustling with activity. Some were military, wearing a mixture of uniforms and whatever the hell they could scavenge. Some were working on the Hawks, others on the convoy vehicles. Civvies were mingling here and there. He saw some kids running around, kicking a soccer ball.

Shaw envied them being able to find some fucking semblance of normality and enjoyment in the middle of chaos.

Reed slapped him on the back and headed off to find his fiancée, Natalya. The energy scientist would probably be helping the geek squad somewhere. Gabe gave him a solemn nod and followed the others. Hell, even big, deadly, and not-very-talkative Gabe had a woman of his own—the sexy and smart head of the medical team, Dr. Emerson Green.

"Get some sleep, Shaw," Marcus said.

"I'm going to check in with the drone operators and see if they've spotted anything—"

Marcus scowled. "You mean bug them until they bug me to get you off their backs."

Shaw slung his rifle over his shoulder. "Whatever it takes."

"You're running on fumes, Baird. Get some rest, or you'll be no help to her." With one hard look, Marcus strode away, no doubt to drag Elle back to their makeshift quarters. Marcus never missed a chance to get his woman naked.

Shaw had been happy for his squad mates, as they'd all found women who gave them some good in the bad. He'd always preferred to enjoy the variety the single ladies offered, rather than tie himself down. He didn't want someone dependent on him, waiting for him to screw up.

He was good at screwing up when it mattered.

But now, watching the guys go, he felt a flash of envy. There were women waiting for his friends, to hold them tight and make them feel better for a little while.

He rubbed a tired hand over his face. He'd give anything right now to have Claudia beside him, ribbing him about being a crap shot or about one of his latest sexual escapades.

He headed back toward one of the converted buses that were filled with bunks for the single squad soldiers. Marcus was right. He'd barely had more than a couple of hours of sleep over the last few days, and if they got a lead on where the raptors had Claudia, they'd need to move fast.

But he was still going to check in with the drone operators, first.

He rubbed at his face again and realized he'd cut himself on something. He'd thought his temple had been damp with sweat, but it was blood. He rubbed it between his fingers, and thought again of those bloodstains on the concrete at that factory.

Someone moved up beside him. "Hey, Shaw."

He looked down and saw Liberty. The curvy blonde was gorgeous, and made no bones about the fact she loved sex. Most people looked at Liberty and didn't see beyond the beauty. But Shaw knew she worked just as hard as the squads behind the scenes to keep the convoy survivors calm and in good spirits. He'd heard that if you needed shampoo, soap, lotion, or—for those whose contraceptive implants had stopped functioning—condoms, Liberty could get her hands on it.

Liberty offered him a smile designed to send all the blood in a man's body south. "I've arranged to have the truck I share with some of the other single ladies to myself for the next hour." Her smile widened and her hand stroked down his arm. "I thought you might like to keep me company."

Casual sex wasn't frowned on like it once had been. Since most people had lost their loved ones in the invasion, sex was a way to get skin-to-skin with someone and hold on tight. To find some laughs in the darkness and not feel so alone.

For some, for him, it had always been about outrunning the darkness and the memories for a few hours.

Now, Liberty's nice little offer, something that he would have been all over a week ago, made his stomach turn over.

"No."

She frowned at him, and Shaw rubbed the back of his neck.

"Sorry. I'm tired and hot and dirty…"

She smiled. "It's okay." She touched his arm again, her expression becoming concerned. "You haven't found Claudia yet?"

Just hearing her name made his throat go tight. He shook his head.

Liberty's fingers tightened on his arm. "Hang in there, Shaw."

He didn't even watch her go. His gaze turned inward. It wasn't him who had to hang in there, it was Claudia.

Shaw turned and headed toward the bus the drone operators used.

Hell Squad

Marcus

Cruz

Gabe

Reed

Roth

Noah

Shaw

Holmes

MORE ACTION ROMANCE?

ACTION
ADVENTURE
TREASURE HUNTS
SEXY SCI-FI ROMANCE

When astro-archeologist and museum curator Dr. Lexa Carter discovers a secret map to a lost old Earth treasure—a priceless Fabergé egg—she's excited at the prospect of a treasure hunt to the dangerous desert planet of Zerzura. What she's not so happy about is being saddled with a bodyguard—the museum's mysterious new head of security, Damon Malik.

After many dangerous years as a galactic spy, Damon Malik just wanted a quiet job where no one tried to kill him. Instead of easy work in a museum full of artifacts, he finds himself on a backwater planet babysitting the most infuriating woman he's ever met.

She thinks he's arrogant. He thinks she's a trouble-magnet. But among the desert sands and ruins, adventure led by a young, brash treasure hunter named Dathan Phoenix, takes a deadly turn. As it becomes clear that someone doesn't want them to find the treasure, Lexa and Damon will have to trust each other just to survive.

The Phoenix Adventures
Among Galactic Ruins
At Star's End
In the Devil's Nebula
On a Rogue Planet
Beneath a Trojan Moon
Beyond Galaxy's Edge
On a Cyborg Planet
Return to Dark Earth
On a Barbarian World
Lost in Barbarian Space

Also by Anna Hackett

Hell Squad
Marcus
Cruz
Gabe
Reed
Roth
Noah
Shaw
Holmes

The Anomaly Series
Time Thief
Mind Raider
Soul Stealer
Salvation
Anomaly Series Box Set

The Phoenix Adventures
Among Galactic Ruins
At Star's End
In the Devil's Nebula
On a Rogue Planet
Beneath a Trojan Moon
Beyond Galaxy's Edge
On a Cyborg Planet
Return to Dark Earth
On a Barbarian World
Lost in Barbarian Space

Perma Series
Winter Fusion

The WindKeepers Series
Wind Kissed, Fire Bound
Taken by the South Wind
Tempting the West Wind
Defying the North Wind
Claiming the East Wind

Standalone Titles
Savage Dragon
Hunter's Surrender
One Night with the Wolf

Anthologies
A Galactic Holiday
Moonlight (UK only)
Vampire Hunter (UK only)
Awakening the Dragon (UK Only)

About the Author

I'm a USA Today bestselling author and I'm passionate about *action romance*. I love stories that combine the thrill of falling in love with the excitement of action, danger and adventure. I'm a sucker for that moment when the team is walking in slow motion, shoulder-to-shoulder heading off into battle.

I write about people overcoming unbeatable odds and achieving seemingly impossible goals. I like to believe it's possible for all of us to do the same.

My books are mixture of action, adventure and sexy romance and they're recommended for anyone who enjoys fast-paced stories where the boy wins the girl at the end (or sometimes the girl wins the boy!)

For release dates, action romance info, free books, and other fun stuff, sign up for the latest news here:

Website: AnnaHackettBooks.com

Printed in Great Britain
by Amazon

86847539R00130